LEAVING THE BRONX

... and what led up to it

A Novel

ZEE ABRAMS

Book Cover and design by Big Pixel Designs

Parkway Publishing
Printed in the United States of America.

Praise for **LEAVING THE BRONX**

"Wonderfully vivid, spot-on memories and terrific dialogue"

   - **Richard Lederer,** newspaper columnist and best-selling author of 50 books about language, history, and humor, including "Comma Sense" and the "Anguished English" series.

Dedicated to my grandchildren......

And to my husband and children for their support

"Unless we remember, we cannot understand."

E. M. Forster

TABLE OF CONTENTS

PART II

PROLOGUE

English 1

The Snow
(A Pivotal Moment in My Life)
Fern Bookman

"Is the sun out?" my mother used to say. "Then go out and get some fresh air! Stay in front of the house," she would add. We lived in a safe neighborhood, but it was still New York City.

My mother always kept my little brother inside with her, but I, on the other hand, was told to go out and play every day, even when it was freezing. I loved to draw and would have preferred to stay inside but was forced to stay out till dark. Compared to our small apartment though, the street wasn't that bad. I learned every detail of the ornamental entrance of the building across the street, and I constructed scenarios about the people going in and out. I think it made me observant and imaginative.

Six story apartment buildings lined our block, and there were usually scores of kids, but when there was nobody around it was torture being anchored to my spot on the stoop.

That morning, I stepped out of the dark lobby of the building and was transfixed. The snow had finally stopped but was everywhere. It was a universe of brightness that subsumed the streets, the cars, and the buildings. Even the sky was a translucent shell. Not a person in sight, no sounds, not even the chirp of a bird - just an eerie silence.

I gasped at the frigid air. It was so cold it had a physical presence. How could life sustain itself? If I stepped too close, I could vanish in the ten-foot snowbanks left by the snowplows. No one would know.

With trepidation I went back to the apartment.

"Did you put rouge on your face?" my mother asked. "Did you take it from my bag?" She had said this before, but I was only eight and not even sure what rouge was.

"How could I do that?" I asked. "I would never take something from your bag!"

"But your face is so red."

Didn't she know it was freezing outside?

"Is the sun out?" she said. There was no refuting that, so back I trudged.

Resigned to my fate, I surveyed the scene. It was the first New York City blizzard in fifty years. The surface of the snow glittered with crystals that almost stabbed the eye. Overnight, my noisy, busy street was transformed into a silent dream world. I inhaled and found the air sweet. I felt like I was taking my first true breath.

Mother Nature, which had never noticed my street before, was making up for her oversight. I was enthralled, awash with intense delight. I knew someday I would paint that feeling.

After a while though, perhaps half an hour, everything changed. The bright, glowing world became mottled with darkness. I saw spots of red and green, but in that wonder-world of newness, I doubted my sensations. Something was wrong!

Finally, I could take it no more - I was going blind. The best experience of my life had become the worst. How could I be an artist now? What would become of me? Frantically, I ran into the building, knowing the way by heart.

My mother explained it was snow-blindness caused by the swelling of the capillaries in the eyes. I kept my eyes shut for ten minutes and drank the hot chocolate my mother made.

I had won a reprieve that day; I wouldn't have to go out again. It seemed forever for my sight to return, but I was sitting in a warm kitchen with my mother by my side.

1

In the years after WWII, Americans like Ann and Leo Bookman were getting on with their lives. They were overjoyed
to be expecting their first child. That child would be named
after great grandfather Ferris. If it was a girl, "Fern," the name
of their ten year old niece, would do. Thus, for years to come,
at family gatherings Fern was always called "Little Fern," even
though she grew tall.

Three years later, Donald was born. Their family now complete, Ann and Leo hired a professional photographer to come to
their apartment. Dressed in their best, they stood around a table
where the baby boy was positioned comfortably.

"Be proud you're a big sister now," her mother said, and Fern
smiled uncertainly. She felt important but a little confused.

Fern wanted to hold her brother for one picture, but Leo said
no. Polio was sweeping the country, and he worried she might,
in some way, infect the baby.

In the photographs, a white screen conceals the apartment.
It was just as well. Small and dark, it was on the ground floor of a
six-story building. The entrance was under the stairwell, and its
three rooms faced an alley. Whoever designed the place wasn't
thinking about the future inhabitants.

Pelham Parkway, the Bookman's working-class neighborhood, was in the northeast Bronx. As the neighborhood devel-
oped, a road was built to connect it with the rest of the Bronx.
That road, Pelham Parkway, lent its name to the neighborhood.

In the 1950's, Bronx neighborhoods were as distinct as

towns across the American prairie. The West Bronx had the Grand Concourse modeled on the Champs Elysee, Arthur Avenue was like a little Italian village, and Parkchester was built by an insurance company. Only Pelham Parkway had a park running through it - a broad swath of green a block wide, separating the parkway's east and west-bound lanes. This grassy area was the neighborhood park where people escaped their apartments to sit in the sun. It was one of the main reasons Leo and Ann loved the neighborhood.

Like many areas of New York, Pelham Parkway was a gateway for immigrants. From across Europe they came, bringing their old ways. In the morning, the clip-clop of the milk-wagon horse could be heard; in the afternoon, it was the cry of the ragman as he walked through the alley.

"I cash clothes, I cash old clothes," the old man cried out, his accent so thick, it sounded like a foreign tongue.

Whole, extended families lived in Pelham Parkway as well as people from the same European towns and areas. It was like a small Jewish town in Europe where everyone knew each other - an American shtetl. It belonged more to the old world than the new, which gave it a charm.

It wasn't uncommon to chat with the stranger sitting next to you on the park bench; no one was a total stranger. It would turn out that this unknown person knew your aunt or lived in the same building as your friend.

Leo was a college graduate, and Ann was soon to get a good job. That should have raised their living standard, but they lived more poorly than most. Though cramped like rabbits in a hutch, they were grateful just to have an apartment, especially one that was rent-controlled. Raised in poverty, they had struggled through the depression and were used to making do. Ann grew up in East Harlem in an apartment behind her father's store, and Leo, in a tenement on the Lower East Side. To them, Pelham Parkway was a piece of heaven.

` ` ` ` `

"You can stay inside with me today," Ann said, as she cleaned the breakfast dishes one winter morning. "It's too cold to go out."

Fern was glad of that. She was poised to draw at the little kitchen table, but there was no paper. Ann took a supermarket bag and cut it in squares. Fern would have preferred white, but brown made a good background too.

"I hate the color of the walls," she said as she picked up a bright green crayon.

"I didn't choose it," Ann said sharply, "It's the landlord's army surplus paint. We could buy our own paint, but I'm not wasting money on that. We're saving to buy our own house."

"But it looks like worms crawling under the paint!" Fern said. She was referring to the rough texture of the walls.

"We're lucky to have this place. Soldiers are returning and there aren't enough apartments. People even bribe the supers. Besides, that texture used to be considered elegant!"

Fern wasn't sure what that meant, but she was sure her mother was wrong. The apartment was right over the basement with its garbage cans, and no matter how much Ann cleaned, there were roaches. Fern was sure theirs was the worst apartment in the building. It was a constant reminder of poverty.

As Fern drew and Ann worked in the kitchen, the baby slept, and there was a companionable silence. When her mother asked if she'd like to go with her to get the mail, Fern agreed. She was glad to get out, even just to walk through the dim lobby.

At the building's entrance, they saw the mailman putting letters into small dark boxes lining the wall. Fern was surprised that it looked like the inside of a beehive. So that's what was behind the little shiny doors she passed every day!

As they waited for the mailman to finish, a girl and her mother came into the building. Fern knew who the girl was, but there was no greeting. It was the same with most of the people in the building. Living so close to hundreds of people, it was important to keep some distance to preserve privacy.

On the walk back to the apartment, Fern thought about all the doors in the building - all shut tight. Beyond those doors were people she sometimes saw but didn't know and rooms she could only imagine.

Her best friend had lived next door from the time she was a baby, and their doors had always been open. It had been almost a year since her friend moved away, and she missed going back and forth between the apartments all day. Now the doors were closed forever.

"Will I ever find another friend?" Fern asked. "There are no girls my age in the building!"

"Don't worry," Ann said. "You'll make plenty of friends when you start school."

"But that's a long time!" Fern complained. Back at her drawing, Fern tried to draw a horse. "Mommy, could I get a horse?" she asked.

Ann laughed. "A horse! Where would you keep it? There's no room in an apartment!" Fern thought the broad alley behind the building would be suitable.

"People in cities don't have horses," Ann explained, "they're only on farms, but how about a dog? "

"Oh, yes, a dog," Fern said, excitedly.

"As soon as we move, we'll get one," Ann promised.

"I can't draw a horse, what should I draw?"

"Draw anything, draw a design," Ann suggested.

Fern made looping scribbles and colored them in. She chose purple, a color she had never used before. When she put dark green next to it, both colors looked brighter. With all the beautiful colors in the world, why was the color of her world army green?

Through the window of her bedroom, Fern could see the fire-escape. Iron bars blocked the window, making the room look like a prison.

"You must never go on the fire-escape, it's dangerous," Ann often reminded her, despite the window being locked. Fern never even went into the room during the day, but she thought about the fire-escape a lot, especially in December. The song about Rudolph, the red-nosed reindeer was a favorite, and she wondered why Santa never came to her home. She had mixed feelings about it because if he landed on the fire-escape, the reindeer's hooves would get caught; it was the reindeers she cared about. Now she asked her mother about it.

"I was meaning to tell you," Ann said. "There really is no Santa Claus."

"Why didn't you tell me? What about the reindeers? Fern asked in astonishment.

"I know," Ann said sheepishly, "I should have told you."

"So there are no reindeers?"

"There are reindeer, but they live in the far north, and they don't fly."

＼ ＼ ＼ ＼ ＼

As Fern got older, sharing the bedroom with her brother became a problem. At night, sensitive to light, she wanted the door closed, but Don wanted the light from the hallway. Every night, in and out of bed they traipsed, closing and opening the door until, exhausted, they finally fell asleep.

Fern's frustration peaked when a friend of Ann's gave her and her brother almost identical cartoon posters of an elephant and a rhinoceros. Fern loved the silly smiles and pink garlands on their heads.

"Which do you want?" Ann asked, holding them up.

"I want the elephant," Fern said promptly.

"I want the elephant too," Don echoed.

Ann reminded Fern that she was the big sister, and Fern agreed to take the other one. Then a curious thing happened; she discovered she liked the rhinoceros better.

" I like the rhinoceros better too," Don said.

"You're just copying me," Fern said furiously.

"You don't deserve them, either of you, so I'm giving them to some other children who do!" Ann exclaimed, and they never saw the posters again.

There were only three pictures in the apartment - two Winslow Homer water-color prints in the living room and a small painting of a brown vase with red poppies in the hallway. Ann told Fern she had painted it in an adult education class before Fern was born, but she had done a much better painting that was in the closet. She couldn't hang it because it was big and you weren't allowed to make holes in the wall.

"Could I see it?" Fern asked excitedly.

"It's in the back of the closet, and I don't have time to take it out now," Ann said, but several days later she cleaned out the closet and did take it out. She held it up proudly. It was a forest scene at dusk in shades of blue, green, and brown. It was the most beautiful painting Fern had ever seen.

"I think I'll give it to my friend Jeanette," Ann said. "I need a nice present for when she moves to Chappaqua."

"Don't give it away!" Fern protested. "Why can't we keep it?"

"It's not doing any good stuck in the closet, and who knows when we'll move?"

They were starved for beauty in that apartment: the walls, the furniture, even the olive colored melmac dishes were drab. The little painting in the hallway, though not beautiful, was hopeful.

2

The highlight of Fern's day was when her father came home. Leo worked at the General Post Office and took a bus and train from 34th Street. He usually came home a little after six. After six-thirty, the minutes ticked by, and Ann became tense. At a quarter to seven, the sound of the key in the lock was a relief.

"Daddy's home, Daddy's home!" Fern and Don would cry out.

Leo had a degree in chemistry and wanted to be a doctor, but his family's poverty forced him to work in the Post Office. When he realized that becoming a doctor was impossible, he studied to be an accountant like his older brother. He was about to take the exam when his brother died of the accountant's disease, a heart attack. Leo was so shaken that he gave up the idea of becoming an accountant and remained with his safe job - he would take no chances. Immigrants who barely spoke English ended up owning factories and businesses, but educated as he was, Leo plodded on at the Post Office. He also had a part-time job, seasonal work in his uncle's fur business. Though he disliked the work, he could laugh about it. At the dinner table, he told "furrier jokes" to his family, and they laughed more at the crudeness of those who told them than the jokes themselves. Mostly, he talked about his Post Office experiences as a packaging specialist, visiting businesses and universities, advising how to ship aerosol cans, explosive chemicals, and even animals.

Once, Leo visited a big company that needed advice on shipping a new product - a spray can of cheese. He gave the sample to Fern and Don to try, and they took turns squirting the cheese which looked like little yellow worms. The whole family laughed at the thought that anyone would buy such a thing.

At bedtime, while Ann cleaned up, Leo told Fern and Don stories about Tom Sawyer. When the stories gave out, they pestered him for more, and he made them up.

On Sunday mornings, Leo took Fern to Snowflake bakery for freshly baked rye bread. It was the best bakery in the neighborhood, and there was always a line snaking out the door, mostly men sent by their wives for a special bread or cake. Even on wintry days, bundled in overcoats, they came for a taste of the old country. They were regulars who knew one another, and they talked in a jocular manner.

"Seeded or plain?" the saleswoman cried out.

Fern pressed her face to the glass display case and admired the beautiful confections: glistening eclairs, powdered Linzer tortes, petits fours, black and whites, and Chinese cookies. Cakes were frosted, fruit-topped and iced, and some had delicate writing on shiny chocolate squares. Who bought those cakes? She never saw one in her house.

The baker from the back of the store yelled, "No more rye, and we're all out of babka!"

"So there's no more rye! Don't get excited, we won't starve!" an old man on line assured his grumbling companions.

Leo was a head taller than the others, and though his features were ordinary, he was striking. Her mother said he looked like Gary Cooper. He didn't yell across the counter or jostle, and standing next to him in the crowded store, Fern was filled with pride.

On the way home, Fern ate the treat Leo always bought her, a swirl of whipped cream with a cherry on top called a Charlotte Russe.

In college, Leo had been an all-around athlete. He could swim, box, play basketball and tennis, but now his main physical activity was walking. He could go for miles without getting tired.

On Sunday afternoons,he took the children on outings so Ann had time to herself. On a sunny fall day, they went to the Bronx Botanical Gardens, a twenty-minute walk from their apartment. They entered through a rear gate on Fordham Road and were immediately surrounded by New York City's last remaining stand of virgin forest.

As they walked, Leo named every tree, and Fern thought him the smartest father in the world.

"This is an oak," he said, bending to pick up a long brown leaf, "and that big spreading tree is a beech. That's an ash, and that one's a maple, but there are many kinds of maple."

Leo loved the woods and was never so at ease as on those walks. He took deep breaths and seemed to expand with each long stride. His children struggled to keep up.

Sometimes he talked about getting a farm. He was born on a farm in Romania, but he barely remembered it. His father, Jacob, managed the farm and might have stayed and raised his family, but Jews weren't allowed to own land or even be farmers.

America was the "goldene medina," a place with unlimited opportunity, but when Jacob got there, he went from being the manager of a prosperous farm to being a peddler on the Lower East Side. Somehow, he managed to raise seven children and send two sons to college.

Leo led Fern and Don on a narrow path along the Bronx River which led to The Old Snuff Mill, a wooden structure from colonial times. A small exhibit next to the mill explained that the British, during the Revolutionary War, wasted time building a bridge only to discover that the Bronx River was only a wide stream. That extra time allowed Washington's troops to escape and eventually win the war.

As Fern watched the water wheel turn, she gazed across the river and pictured the Redcoats threading their way through the dense, green forest.

In the museum, Leo read aloud the inscription on a detailed diorama of the colonial Bronx.

NEW YORK was originally a DUTCH outpost. In 1642, JONAS BRONCK came from HOLLAND and bought a large piece of land from the LENAPE INDIANS. He built a farm by a river which came to be known as BRONCK'S RIVER. When people travelled there, they said they were going to the BRONCK'S.

In time, the whole area came to be known as THE BRONCKS. In 1697, the legislature simplified the spelling to THE BRONX.

3

In kindergarten, when asked what she wanted to be when she grew up, Fern said, "The President's wife."

Theo, a boy Fern liked, said he wanted to be President. He had freckles, a ruddy complexion and a quick smile. He paired up with her in the basket-weaving corner, and she prepared meals for him on the toy stove in the playhouse. Every day she looked forward to seeing him at school, but after kindergarten he moved away. She never liked any other boy at school as much.

By second grade, Fern started walking to school by herself. It was only two blocks, and Ann was busy with Don. As she came to the end of the block where Netherland Avenue met Lydig Avenue, Fern saw a tiny girl hurrying out of a building. If such a small girl could go to school by herself, so could she. There were lots of people around: men rushing to the train, shopkeepers opening stores, and women shopping.

As Fern approached P.S. 303, children and mothers came streaming from all sides. The school was a massive brick building that filled an entire block. Everyone lined up in the yard every day, even in freezing weather. Only when it rained were they allowed to line up inside.

Fern took her place on line, eager for the day to start. She saw others hurrying to get into line before the whistle blew. At the shrill blast, a girl came rushing into the yard, her school bag flying. A teacher grabbed her and motioned her to the wall.

"Stand there! You're late - we need to get your name."

Fern marched inside with her class and looked back at the girl, pressed against the brick wall. She looked so forlorn. That will never be me, Fern vowed.

Fern loved everything about school except lining up. As soon as she entered the building, she had a feeling of well-being. Reproductions of Impressionist paintings lined the main hallway. "Girls at the Piano," by Renoir was her favorite. The pastel greens and blues were softer than any colors she had ever seen; she wished she could be in that room. On the upper floors, bright bulletin boards punctuated the walls of wide hallways. Linoleum floors were so highly polished, it was a treat to walk on them. The students and all the people who worked their took pride in the school.

Silence reigned in the corridors. Only faint sounds escaped sturdy wooden classroom doors. Inside the rooms, students obediently copied from the blackboard.

In P.S. 305, every room was a universe of calm and order. It was as strict as a parochial school. The principal, assistant principal, and many teachers were unmarried women devoting their lives to other people's children.

"Boys and girls, get ready," the teacher said every morning.

Students put their books and pencil cases inside their desks and looked up. With folded hands on their desks, they looked to the boxlike loudspeaker mounted high above the teacher's desk.

"Good morning boys and girls, this is Miss Monahan," came the stern, clear voice of the principal. So focused were the students, it was as if Miss Monahan herself hovered over the box.

The principal was more of an idea than an actual physical presence. She kept to her office, but her name was always on teachers' lips.

"Don't talk in the hallways, don't go up the down staircase, don't run in the halls, Miss Monahan will be angry!"

For real misbehavior, there was a worse threat - the permanent record card. Every report card was part of the permanent record which followed you for life.

The school's hierarchy started at the Board of Education at

110 Livingstone Street in Brooklyn. From there, it descended like a pyramid to the district offices, the principals, assistant principals, and finally the teachers. Student monitors lorded over other students, who themselves were ranked academically.

Six classes on every grade were grouped homogenously. The same groups stayed together in classes from year to year, with other students non-existent in their world. Fern's classes were the first or second on the grade. When she was put in class 3-2 rather than 3-1, she comforted herself that Kay, the neighborhood doctor's brilliant daughter, was there too.

Like every New York City elementary school, there was assembly on Friday mornings. White shirts and blouses with ties or scarfs in the school color were required. At P.S. 303, the color was green, but other schools had red or blue.

The program began with the school anthem, whose words had been written by Miss Monahan.

"Dear 303, we sing of you/ Our hearty praises ring for you/ We'll help to raise your standards high/ And spread your good name far and wide...."

The separation of church and state was strictly observed: there were no Christmas trees or carols. Many of the children had relatives murdered by the Nazis, so there was an aversion to anything German, yet the children sang fervently, innocent that the tune was that of "Oh Tannenbaum", a German Christmas song.

Fern attended P.S. 303 for seven years and never spoke to the principal except once in second grade. Returning from the girls' room, she saw a tall, distinguished-looking woman. She immediately knew who it was, but before she could open the classroom door, the words: "Little girl!" rang out.

"Would you please tell me what time it is? My watch stopped," the principal said.

Fern opened the classroom door and looked at the clock at the front of the room. One hand was on the ten, another on the two. She stared for a moment, hoping for an epiphany. If she took too long, it would give her away – she couldn't tell time!

She took a guess and said "Ten to two."

Miss Monahan, apparently satisfied, walked away, but Fern slunk to her seat. Even if she guessed right, she had lied. As soon as she got home, she would learn to tell time. But for days, she was alert whenever the teacher looked her way or someone came to the classroom door.

` ` ` ` `

On Fern's walk home from school she paused at the corner of busy Lydig Avenue. On sunny days, even in cold weather, people brought folding chairs just to sit on the street and watch the colorful scene. There was a kosher butcher, a fish store, two delicatessens, two bakeries, a candy store, an old general store, and a new supermarket. At the large fruit and vegetable market that spilled onto the street, men with fur-lined Russian hats and women with babushkas squeezed the produce to make sure it was fresh.

"Leave those oranges alone!" the white-aproned store owner shouted.

In the stores were handmade cheeses, kugels, and fish that was smoked, chopped, or marinated. Shopkeepers took pride in preparing food the old way, and Yushke was the most old-fashioned of all. Fern liked to go into his store which was like the general stores in Western movies. Everything was wood - the long high counter, the buckled floor, warped shelves, and big pickle barrels. Fern sometimes bought a pickle as an after-school treat, and Yushke himself, large and genial with a starched white apron, came from behind the counter to fish out a "special sour one" from the pickle-barrel. The new Daitch supermarket, a block away, was drawing business away, and the store was empty.

Fern watched as Yushke carefully wrap the dripping pickle in wax paper and graciously handed it to her. If I had a grandfather, she thought, I would want him to be like that.

4

When it was warm, the women of Fern's building brought folding chairs to the street. They chatted and watched their children play. Some set up mah-jong tables right on the sidewalk.

As Fern went into the building, conversation stopped and she felt their eyes on her. Ann called the women "yentas." They should have been working at a job, or doing housework. She thought they were wasting time. She had nothing to do with them.

"Stay on the stoop until other children come out to play," Ann told Fern.

The stoop, a long, low step that ran along the front of the building was the city's front porch.

On a sunny, spring day, there were already boys and girls standing on the stoop when Fern went out. They were getting ready for a special game called "God." When Morty, a tall boy, a policeman's son, called your name you were allowed to take a step off the stoop. Morty preferred to play ball, and the kids were excited he deigned to play with them, but as soon as he saw his friends, he left.

Fern and three other girls decided to jump rope, but first they had to choose who would turn the rope.

"Eeny,meeny,miney,mo," a girl sang out, then pointed to Fern.

After ten minutes, Fern got her turn to jump, but ten minutes later, the girls tired of jump-rope, and a game of ring-a-lievio was organized which included the boys on the street. It was hide-and-seek with teams; one team hid, each child separately, while the other searched.

As Fern crouched in the alley, unsure whether, in that dark place, she wanted to be found or not, she was scared but excited. She had heard about the bogey-man, but she didn't know if it was real. If there was something to be afraid of, why would her parents allow such a game? On the other hand, she guessed they didn't even know about it.

In good weather, there were always children around, but on a foot freezing, skin tingling day, Fern stood alone on the stoop. Adults went in and out as she huddled against the building to keep warm. Then another girl, new to the building, came and stood beside her.

"Did you just move in?" Fern asked.

"Yes," the girl answered. "We're on the fourth floor, what floor are you ?"

"The ground floor," Fern said, wondering if the girl, who was younger, understood the fourth floor was considered better. She was too young to be a potential friend anyhow. The girl annoyed her as she boasted about the new furniture her mother had bought. Finally, more interested in the apartment than the furniture, Fern asked to see it.

As they rode up in the elevator, Fern envisioned a room gleaming with newness, and the living room was as nice as she expected. There were two large windows, plush furniture and a Persian style rug. Fern was entranced, but as she took a step into the living room, the girl cautioned, "Don't go in! My mother said no children allowed because of the new furniture."

Fern noticed the plastic covers and remembered her mother saying, "Why buy velvet furniture only to cover it with plastic?" From that moment,she lost interest in seeing other apartments.

When Fern returned to her own apartment, Ann made hot chocolate and watched her drink.

"I hope you're not coming down with another sore throat; the doctor says you should have your tonsils out."

"It's not so bad," Fern answered quickly. "My throat feels better now. I don't want my tonsils out!"

In those days, most children had their tonsils removed. An economical method had been devised for working-class families - thirty children at a time went to a clinic and, in assembly line style, had the operation. They stayed overnight in a dormitory at the clinic.

When Ann proposed it, Fern was frantic with fear - she had never spent a night away from her family. Ann assured her she would be the first mother there in the morning. She promised over and over until Fern agreed.

After the operation, Fern lay in the dark dormitory with children moaning on all sides. Her throat burned and some children were crying, but she just had to get through the night. Her mother would be the first one in the morning.

That morning, a nurse brought the children to a large reception room to wait. All eyes were on the door. The first mother was not Fern's, nor were the next who followed in quick succession. They came bearing dolls, teddy bears, and ice cream.

Finally, Fern blurted out: "I thought my mother was going to be first. That's what she said!" A sad looking boy said his mother told him the same thing. They couldn't all be first, but as the room emptied, Fern's anger turned to fear.

What if her mother wasn't coming? What if she was in an accident or had never been planning to come at all? Perhaps the clinic was a place to leave unwanted children.

"Where's my mother?" Fern asked the nurse. "She said she would be first!"

Instead of answering, the nurse loudly addressed the remaining children. "What's wrong with your mothers? Did they forget about you? "

Fern watched the big clock on the wall; she had never known how slowly the hands on a clock could move.

When Ann finally appeared, Fern couldn't look at her. Ann mumbled an excuse about an errand that took longer than expected.

"I'm sorry," she said."I'll get you an ice cream to make up for it."

Fern bitterly remembered her mother had promised ice cream before the operation.

5

For most of the year they lived like paupers, but in the summer the Bookmans felt like kings when they escaped the city for the beach. Rockaway, at the end of the subway line, had clean, sandy beaches and the pure waters of the Atlantic. In the late 1800s, vacationers came to its hotels, but now it was old and dilapidated.

The Bookmans rented ramshackle bungalows or apartments in rambling old houses, whatever they could find. Like their apartment on Netherland Avenue, the place where they sheltered didn't matter. Their real living was done outside: in Rockaway they lived at the beach.

Each morning, Ann packed a big beach bag and lunch. The beach was practically empty at that hour, and she had a choice of where to set down her blanket. It had to be far enough from the shoreline to avoid the rising tide but close enough to keep her eye on Don.

Fern was in charge when Ann went for her swim. Back and forth beyond the surf, almost beyond sight, she did a perfect Australian crawl. It was what she lived for.

"She's a good swimmer, a very good swimmer," seven-year-old Fern told herself, but for twenty minutes she kept her eyes on the bobbing white bathing cap far from shore. Only when her mother came out of the water, shaking herself like a wet seal, did Fern relax.

"Now you two can play in the sand," Ann said, and Fern and Don ran to the water's edge.

Four-year-old Don started scooping wet sand into his pail, and Fern stood in the shallow water gazing towards the horizon. She thought about England on the other side. It was too far to see, but perhaps she would spot a three-masted ship like the one Columbus or the Pilgrims sailed.

Don tried to build Mayan temples and Persian palaces like the ones he had seen in Leo's college textbook on ancient civilizations. He could spend hours manipulating the wet sand into building blocks, arches and ramps. He was amazingly skillful. Fern returned to the blanket.

"Why don't you play with Don? You used to love to build sandcastles," Ann said, annoyed.

But Fern was too old for that, and she was glad to have her mother all to herself.

Ann stood up to check on Don. More people had arrived, partially obscuring her line of sight, but Don's curly brown head was distinctive.

On a nearby blanket, a woman had a white and tan terrier on a tight leash. She was feeding it little treats from a bag, but when she turned away for a moment, the dog stuck its muzzle in the bag. Ann and Fern laughed.

"Will I ever get a dog?" Fern asked.

"Don't you remember? I promised you could when we move."

"But what if we never move?"

The dog, seeing endless space, strained to get free, and the woman, turning towards them, said, "If I let him go, he'd run away."

The sun was beginning to set, and people were leaving the beach. It was time to go home. Ann went to get Don, but when she got to the water's edge she saw the little curly head, the one she had been watching for so long, was not Don's! She had been watching the wrong child. Frantically, she scanned the now deserted beach. Don was nowhere in sight.

Ann and Fern looked in the dark space under the boardwalk and then on the next section of beach. They called to Don until they were hoarse. Alone on the endless stretch of sand, they sensed the danger of the beach. The waves licked the shore with little devil tongues.

Fern was frightened. She thought of her father's rage when he found out. Whatever happened, their lives would never be the same. They were guilty: her mother for lack of attention, and she for distracting her. If Don was really gone, all their happiness would also be gone.

Finally, Ann called the police. They came and spread out to comb the beaches. Fern and Ann walked along the boardwalk calling Don's name. An hour later, a policeman approached them.

"We're still looking, ma'am," he said. "Why don't you go home, and we'll call as soon as we find him."

When they got home, Ann called Leo at work, but he had already left.

"Are you all right if I leave you? asked Ann. "I'm going back to look. Stay here till I get back."

Fern sat perfectly still on a kitchen chair and watched as the small window grew dark. If she sat perfectly still, perhaps everything would be all right. She tried not to think of a little boy alone on the beach at night.

When she heard steps, her heart lightened. Maybe it's them, she thought. But Ann came in alone. There was no supper, just a glass of milk. Exhausted, Fern fell asleep immdiately and had a nightmare. It wasn't about her brother - she was watching her mother swim far out to sea. Farther and farther she kept swimming.

"Stop," Fern cried out. Then someone was shaking her. It was her father.

"It's all right," he said, smiling. "They found him."

"Where's Mommy?" Fern asked.

"She went to the police station. A lady found Don and took him home."

They never talked about it again. It was as if that day never happened. But Ann never let Don out of her sight again. Until he went away to college, she always knew exactly where he was. Fern, on the other hand, could take care of herself.

6

Leo asked Ann, "Are you almost ready?" He stood at the door with his coat on, hat in hand.

"Almost," Ann said, as she grabbed some apples from a bowl and stuffed them into a small paper bag.

The family walked to the elevated train station on White Plains Road. Almost every Saturday, Fern, her mother and brother took the train five stops downtown to Grandma's, and Leo took the train uptown to the V.A. Hospital to visit his brother Israel.

On the train, Fern and Don knelt on the seats and looked out the window. "Bronx Park East", "180th Street," "Freeman Street," Fern read the station signs. The train ran so close to the buildings they could see into apartments. They saw old furniture, unmade beds, and scantily clad children. A man in a torn undershirt leaned out a window and yelled down to the street.

Going to Grandma's was like visiting a foreign country. Latin music blared from bodegas, street carts sold cuchifritoes, and groups of men sat at little folding tables on the sidewalks playing cards and dominoes. At Easter time, chicks, ducklings, and bunnies filled the pet store window, which Leo said was illegal. The run-down neighborhood was nothing like Pelham Parkway, but Fern liked it.

Grandma's building was old, but vestiges of elegance like the sculpted entrance and marble stairs remained. After climbing four flights, they breathlessly entered the apartment.

It was a different world, peaceful and timeless. Shafts of light from the front window gave the room a soft glow. A bowl of fruit and a sponge cake sat atop a spotless white tablecloth. Everything was clean, spacious, and orderly. Heavy, carved wooden furniture and two small paintings of the woods at sunset were reminders of better times.

"Come in, come in," Grandma said warmly. Her gray hair and shapeless clothing made her look older than she was.

Grandma was Shomer Shabbos. No work was allowed on Saturday, not even turning on a light. Grandma prepared food ahead of time for Saturday. Here, time, meticulously measured during the week, stretched out languorously.

Grandma's orthodox lifestyle was one that Ann and Leo didn't follow. They ate kosher food, never mixing meat with milk, but they didn't have separate dishes, and Ann didn't light candles on Friday night. Ann told Fern they only kept the customs and traditions that were meaningful to them. Some traditions were ingrained though, like not buying baby things before birth. In olden days, giving birth was too dangerous to tempt fate. Ann laughingly told Fern that when she was an infant, they put her in the bottom drawer of the dresser, and because she was so quiet, they almost closed the drawer on her.

A boy, a little older than Don was seated at a large dining table that dominated the living room.

"Olga brought Stanley over this morning," Grandma said.

"She couldn't stop to say hello?" Ann asked sharply. Grandma, resigned to the long-standing rift between her daughters, remained silent.

Ann emptied the bag of apples into a fruit bowl on the table. Next to it were five tiny plastic figures, four dinosaurs and one spaceman.

"Which do you want?" Fern asked the two little boys. She always let them pick first to avoid arguments, and for the next few hours they all played happily, trooping from room to room in a make-believe world.

In the bathroom, when Fern reached for the light switch, a

pile of torn toilet paper reminded her not to. So many things were different at Grandma's.

Neighbors on the way to the fifth and sixth floors stopped at Grandma's door. Though tired after the stairs, it wasn't only refreshment they sought but a calm presence and willingness to listen. At a light knock, Grandma welcomed a tall, stout woman who hesitated when she saw the other guests.

" Come in," Grandma said. "We were just having tea."

The woman didn't stay long, and after she left, Ann asked who she was. Grandma explained she was a Polish woman who stopped in occasionally, and they spoke Polish together.

At another knock, Ann asked, "You're not expecting anyone, are you?"

"They like to stop by on the way up," Grandma said, going to the door.

"I hope I'm not interrupting," a nicely dressed woman said. "I was coming from shul, and I thought I would stop in."

"Anytime, "Grandma said, "anytime!" She introduced the woman as Mrs. Davis, and asked, "How is everything, the family well?"

"Yes, thanks, everyone's well. You know there's a problem with the shul?"

Grandma nodded. "So it's really going to close?"

"Yes," Mrs. Davis said sadly. "People are moving away." "First the butcher, then the chicken market, and now the shul."

"Are there any other Jewish families left in the building?" Ann asked after the woman left.

"There's also the Cohens," Grandma said, "a nice family with a boy and girl. They go to Day School. When we moved here, most of the building was Jewish."

Fern asked if Grandma would take her to shul one day, and Ann looked up in surprise.

"Why do you want to go?" Ann asked; she and Leo never went except on Yom Kippur.

"If she wants to go, I'll take her," Grandma said.

Ann and Grandma sipped their tea in weighty silence.

"You know the other day, I was on my way to shop, and Mrs. Cohen was waiting for the bus with her children. I heard the daughter ask if she was beautiful. She's a smart woman, Mrs. Cohen. You know what she said? 'When you're good, you're beautiful!'"

"That was smart," Ann agreed.

"When you're good, you're beautiful," Grandma repeated, savoring the words.

＼ ＼ ＼ ＼ ＼

Fern looked at the framed photos crowding the top of the bureau in Grandma's bedroom. She was staying overnight - a special treat.

The photos were old, mostly of people Fern didn't know. She loved the wedding photo in which her parents looked like glamorous movie stars. Another photo caught her attention - the only portrait. It was of a good-looking man with a dark handle-bar mustache and a stern expression.

"Who is that?" Fern asked as her grandmother tucked her in. "Is that my grandfather?"

"You don't know?" Grandma exclaimed. "It's not your grandfather, it's your great-grandfather. It's late now, go to sleep, I'll tell you tomorrow."

When Fern slept over, Grandma slept on a daybed in the living room. Her own large, wooden bed had bedposts carved like swans, and it was a treat for Fern to sleep in it.

At home, Ann would say, "Hurry up and go to bed or you'll be late for the feather ball!" At Grandma's, Fern didn't need to be coaxed. She felt like a princess in Grandma's bed. It was marvelous how every feather was delicately carved. Surely, in that bed, she would be transported to the feather ball.

In the morning, Fern asked if Grandma had brought the bed from Europe, and Grandma laughed. They were only allowed a small bag on the ship, she said.

"We brought featherbeds," Grandma explained, "made from tiny hand-plucked goose feathers. It took days to make them; I remember helping when I was a girl. That was all we had to keep warm."

Grandma was quiet for a while, and then at Fern's urging she told about how she came to America.

"I was just a girl, eleven years old. I was a milliner's assistant. Yes, girls that young had to work. Kolo was a small town in Russia/Poland. They let us keep the stores open Sunday mornings.

"It was Easter, and I was just leaving. They came from the farms, the peasants. They were in wagons, with pitchforks and shovels. They were shouting, "death to the Jews, death to the Christ killers." They were throwing stones. Everyone was running. I tried to run, but it was hard with a skirt. Then some Russian soldiers came, but they didn't do anything. They just stood there and watched. Then a stone struck an officer on the forehead and there was blood. He shot into the air, then he ordered them to leave. That Russian soldier saved my life.

"When I got home and told my parents, they decided to send me to America. They saved for five years and sent me with my brother Sam. That's how I came to America. I was sixteen."

When she finished, Grandma went into the kitchen. A few minutes later she brought freshly squeezed orange juice to the table. At home, it came in plastic containers. Grandma continued her story and told how, within a year of her arrival, she married Joseph, a distant cousin. They rented a store in East Harlem that sold mirrors and lampshades and lived in the apartment in the back. Soon she gave birth to a girl, Olga. Five years later Ann was born.

"It wasn't so bad," Grandma said, seeing Fern's expression. "A lot of families lived in the back of the store."

"Who is that man in the photo?" Fern asked. "You said you'd tell me."

"You ask who that is? That's who you're named after! That's Ferris. I'm surprised you didn't know. He was a great man, everybody admired him. Tall and handsome. They took him for the Russian army when he was young. They did that. They took Jewish boys and kept them for twenty-five years.

"Ferris was chosen for the czar's personal cavalry. That was an honor because Jews weren't usually allowed to do that. They let him because he was so good. Most Jewish boys never returned home; they were lost to the Jewish community, but Ferris did go home. He married and had children then brought his family to America. Everyone admired him. That's who you're named after."

It was late in the afternoon when Ann came. She apologized for being late, but Grandma said it was a good thing because she had prepared something for dinner and they could eat together.

"I'll just have some tea," Ann said. "I want to get home before dark."

As they drank, Fern asked if she could someday go to shul with Grandma. She wanted to see it before it closed.

Ann looked startled. "Why do you want to go?"

"It's all right," Grandma said, "I don't know when, but if I can, I'll take her."

"If it's all right with Grandma, you can go," Ann said.

It was already dark, and they hurried through the streets. When they passed the brightly lit pet store, Fern begged, "Can I just take a look?"

"Only for a minute," Ann said.

Scores of chicks and ducklings waddled around in the window - it was Eastertime. Fern longed to hold one even though she remembered that it was wrong to sell them in the city.

Suddenly, Ann yanked her arm. "Let's go."

From the corner of her eye, Fern saw a man behind them. The light from the window gave a glint to his eye.

"Walk fast," Ann commanded.

"I'm walking as fast as I can!" Fern protested.

When they finally got on the train, Ann was tense. Fern listened to the rumbling of the wheels "when you're good, you're beautiful, good, beautiful . . ."

7

Fern listened as her mother worked in the kitchen. Ann sang when she was happy.

"When I was a girl about half-past three/ My mother said Annie, come here to me/ Things may come and things may go/ But here's one thing you ought to know/ It ain't what you do, it's the way that you do it/ And that's what makes things go."

"How can you remember the words to so many songs?" Fern asked.

"I can remember songs, but otherwise I have a very bad memory," Ann answered. "I can see a movie twice without remembering it. It's a terrible fault. It's a good thing your father has a good memory. Otherwise things would fall apart." Ann paused in thought. "There is a good side though - I forget the bad things."

　　＼＼＼＼

That Sunday, Ann decided to forgo housework for a family outing at the zoo.

"How come you're going with us today?" Fern asked." It's always just Daddy."

"I want to go places too. Besides, we haven't seen the new Africa exhibit, and there's a baby giraffe just a few days old."

At the entrance of their building, a pregnant woman in a tent-like dress toddled ahead of them. Fern giggled and said, "She looks like Humpty-Dumpty."

Don laughed.

"That's not nice," Ann reprimanded. "She can't help how she looks. You shouldn't make fun of people."

"I wouldn't say it to her!" Fern protested.

The Farm in the Zoo was Fern's favorite part of the zoo. Petting the animals was allowed, and cats and dogs ran around freely. The resident farmer answered questions, demonstrated how to milk the cows, and how to collect eggs. Fern hoped, some day to stay on a farm.

Later, they saw the seals being fed, visited the Lion House, the aviary, the elephants, and great apes. They ate their lunch on a park bench and slowly wended their way to the African Veldt - the main attraction.

A small crowd stood by the giraffe enclosure. The baby stood on wobbly legs and was almost as tall as Fern.

"How can it be so big?" Fern asked.

"What do you mean?" Ann answered.

"I mean how could something so big get out of its mother's body?"

"You know how," Ann said. "We'll talk about it later."

On the way back, they stopped to rest frequently. Nobody passed them by; they were alone.

"Where is everyone? Are we the only people left?" Fern asked.

Leo looked at his watch. "It's almost five," he said. " Let's walk quickly, the zoo closes soon."

They made their way through empty walkways and broad plazas. Fern walked so fast she got a pain in her side. The sound of a distant howl convinced her not to slow down. Don was even more tired, and Leo carried him on his back for a while.

"Weren't you keeping track of the time?" Ann said to Leo. "We might have trouble getting out."

As they approached the open area by the main gates of the zoo, Fern became afraid. It was deserted, and the gates were closed; it looked like they were trapped. There was a distant howl again, and she pictured a lion walking freely through the zoo.

Did they let the animals out at night? It would be good exercise, and they would be glad to get out of their cages.

The sun was setting and there was a nip in the air. What would they do if they had to spend the night in the zoo?

The main entrance was an iconic bronze gate with massive animals standing twenty feet tall. It was locked, and there was no one in sight.

There was a space between the giant tortoises at the bottom of the gate. Fern suggested they try to squeeze through.

"It's worth a try," Ann said, "but Daddy won't be able to. It's such a small opening."

"It's O.K." Leo said. "If worse comes to worse, I'll manage. I want you and the kids to try."

Leo hoisted Fern onto the tortoise's back, and she worked her way through. It was already dark. She watched tensely as her mother and brother squirmed through with Leo's help.

Her father was much taller and broader, and they anxiously watched as he torturously squeezed his large frame into the narrow opening. Scraped and bruised, he came through.

He threw his arm around Ann and laughed. "I didn't think I'd make it!"

"Neither did I," Ann said. "I'm glad I decided to wear pants today."

On the walk home, Fern thought about how no other family had adventures like hers.

` ` ` ` `

Several days later, as Fern arose from the dinner table, Ann said: "Sit down, we have something we have to talk to you about."

Don had already left the room, and her parents looked very serious. Was it about Don or had Grandma died?

"We're going to tell you about babies. Remember you asked?"

Fern had forgotten her question about the baby giraffe.

She did want to know, but not now, and certainly not with her father there! They hadn't even started talking, and she was embarassed already.

"Daddy and I decided that we should talk to you together,"

Ann began. Leo looked grim.

Ann briefly explained how babies were made, emphasizing the man's part but glossing over what most concerned Fern. How did a large baby get out of a small opening? That was what confused and concerned her.

There was something even more troubling - pajamas.

The apartment was so cold in winter that warm flannel pajamas were necessary. Did you have to take them off? If you did, how did you know when it was the right time?

"Do you have any questions?" her mother asked, but Fern was loathe to prolong the agony. Even if she knew how to ask, she wouldn't have.

For a long time, she couldn't stop thinking about her embarassment in front of her father and the pajamas. She comforted herself that the talk was over and she would never have to go through it again. Someday, when she got married, she wouldn't know what to do. That bothered her the most.

8

Ann put a block of frozen broccoli into a pot of boiling water.

Fern dutifully ate the tasteless food on her plate. She didn't want to hurt her mother's feelings or be reminded of the starving children in China.

"Why do you always get frozen vegetables?" Fern asked.

"I really don't like cooking. If it takes more than ten minutes, I don't do it. I don't want to be in the kitchen while everyone is out doing things. I hate housework, but it has to be done."

Ann pursed her lips. " I might as well tell you now. I'm planning to get a job when Don starts school."

Standing at the kitchen sink filled with soapy water, Ann reached for her rubber gloves. Then she screamed.

"It's gone! My diamond,it's gone!" She held her hand up in disbelief.

"I knew the setting was loose, I should have had it tightened."

Fern had never seen her mother so upset since the day Don disappeared.

"It's my only ring. Daddy gave it to me," Ann said mournfully.

"We'll look for it, but if we don't find it, we'll get Slim." Slim was the super who lived in the basement and could fix anything.

After a fruitless search Ann said, "I'll keep looking, but go get Slim. You know where he lives, it's the door at the end of the basement."

"Why don't you call him?" Fern asked. She didn't want to go.

"I can never get him, he has a party line. Go quick! Tell him to hurry."

Fern had never gone to the basement alone. When she got off the elevator, she looked around. The gray walls were hewn from bedrock, and bare lightbulbs cast eerie shadows. The smell of garbage made her hold her breath, and from the corner of her eye, she saw a mouse scurry along the wall. Panicked, she ran back to the elevator.

"Don't be a sissy!" she told herself and turned back.

At the super's door, she rang the bell. Living in the basement was much worse than she had imagined.

A woman she had never seen before came to the door. Her dark, uncombed hair, made her look like a witch. Fern was expecting Slim, tall, blue-eyed Slim. It took a moment to understand this hawk-faced woman was his wife.

"What do you want?" she asked harshly.

"Is Slim here? My mother needs him. She lost her diamond, and she thinks it went down the drain."

"He's not here. As soon as he comes, I'll tell him."

When Fern got back to the apartment, she told her mother about the mouse. "How can people live like that?" she asked.

"People do. They live in worse places. Maybe now you can see our place isn't so bad."

Fern saw Ann relax as soon as Slim came. There was something wholesome about him with his clean, worn dungarees and the lock of hair that fell in his eyes. He was unlike her father and uncles who could barely wield a hammer. It was a European thing, Ann explained. It was looked down on for a man to have to use his hands. Fern thought that was foolish. Besides, Slim used his head too. How else could he fix the huge boiler in the basement?

Fern couldn't stop thinking about the woman in the basement. How could he have such wife?

" I hope he finds it before Daddy gets home," Ann said.

"Was it worth a lot?" Fern asked.

"It's not that - Daddy gave it to me. It's sentimental."

"It may have gone down the drain," Slim said. "There's nothing more I can do."

When Leo came home, he said it didn't matter. He would get her a new one, but Ann said, "No! No more diamonds."

Fern kept thinking about the ring. "Why aren't you getting another ring? All the other mothers have one."

Ann put down the dish she was drying and sat next to Fern at the kitchen table.

"Did I ever tell you how I met your father? It was during the war. Most of the men were fighting overseas. There weren't any men around. I was twenty-six, and I thought I'd be an old maid."

"What's an old maid?" Fern asked.

"It's when a woman doesn't get married." Ann paused and smiled. "All my friends were married already. I had boyfriends, but I was waiting for the right one. And then there was the war. Anyhow, one night I decided to go to a big dance. There were some men, soldiers on leave and in training, and others who were 4F."

"What's that?"

"That's when there's something wrong with you and they don't want you. It's a good thing I went, because that's where I met Daddy."

Fern had never thought about her parents meeting. It seemed they had always been together.

"I went up to the balcony of the dance hall," Ann continued, "and looked down. I wasn't going down till I saw someone I liked, someone tall, dark, and handsome. Then I saw Daddy. That was my lucky night."

Ann explained that Leo was supposed to report for active duty but was excused at the last minute because of flat feet. He was a very good dancer though, and within a year they were married.

"Neither of us had any money. We were both working to support our families. I didn't want a diamond ring, but Daddy got it for me anyway. That was enough. I didn't need a gold band too."

"Where was the wedding?"

"Didn't I ever tell you about my wedding?" Ann said. "It was actually right across the street in the little shul."

Fern had passed the small, old shul many times; it was hardly noticeable between two large apartment buildings. Her mother's professional wedding pictures made it look like a fancy wedding at the Waldorf Astoria. A long banquet table with a huge flower arrangement had men and women sitting around it in formal attire, the men in black ties, and the women with elegant dresses with corsages.

"But that shul is Orthodox," Fern said.

Ann laughed. "It didn't matter. It was half-price because it was a Tuesday night in February. We didn't have any money. When I got out of the car, there was snow on the ground, and somebody gave me a pair of socks to put over my wedding shoes."

"But your wedding dress was so beautiful. It must have cost a lot!"

Ann laughed again. "No, it didn't cost a thing. I borrowed it, but it fit perfectly." She paused a minute, lost in thought. "Daddy gave me that ring. It had a special meaning. It can never be replaced. I'll just get a plain gold band, and that's it."

＼ ＼ ＼ ＼ ＼

Don just missed the cut-off date for school. He would be a year older than his classmates, yet he refused to go to kindergarten.

The teacher allowed Ann to sit in the classroom the first day and then the second. On the third day, as Don fussed at the classroom door, the teacher said Ann could not stay. If he didn't calm down, he'd have to wait another year.

That afternoon, Ann spoke firmly to Don. He had no choice, he had to go to school. The next day, he stopped protesting. A few days later, when he had settled into the school routine, Ann told Fern, "Now I'll be able to get a job. I'm going to be a school secretary. I'll get home before you, and you won't even know the difference."

"Why do you want a job?" Fern asked. "Isn't it enough to take care of us and Daddy?"

"I can do both. Besides, I'll go crazy staying in this house."

Ann had taken a civil service test and was on a list for school secretaries. She thought it would be a long wait, but her assignment came within the year. It was in a crime-ridden neighborhood in the South Bronx. To get to the school, she would have to walk alone from the subway for five blocks. Leo thought it was too dangerous.

The letter said she could decline the appointment and wait for the next opening. Her friend Nadia, also a school secretary, advised her against it, but Ann accepted. She would start at the beginning of the next school year.

＼ ＼ ＼ ＼ ＼

For Fern, visiting aunt Adele was a treat. The Bookmans always went on the Jewish holidays when school was closed - it was a family tradition.

Leo's sister Adele was a favorite in the family. The oldest girl, as a teenager she had been the first to come to America, bringing with her Abe, her eleven year old brother.

Adele was accomplished in housekeeping, cooking and sewing - she made all her daughter's dresses. Although her husband was a traveling salesman and often away (or maybe because of it), she was a happy woman and rarely left her apartment.

Every time they visited Adele, Fern wished she too lived in Granada Gardens. Only a few blocks away, it was like a different world. Six-story brick buildings surrounded a central garden with trees and walkways. The buildings themselves had Moorish archways and terra-cotta tiles.

Adele's bright, airy sixth floor apartment was the nicest Fern had ever seen. Overstuffed chairs, highly polished furniture, and cut-glass bowls (always full of colorfully wrapped candies) gave it an air of opulence.

Leo beamed, happy that his sister had realized her immigrant dream of a prosperous home. Fern sat at the piano; her aunt had given her permission to touch the keys lightly.

Adele spoke about her son. "I can't control him. He runs around the neighborhood with a group of boys, and I don't know where he goes. My neighbor saw him on the roof the other day."

Fern wasn't surprised that her tall, athletic, fourteen year old cousin preferred the outdoors to his mother's apartment.

"Is that a new chair?" Ann asked, changing the subject.

"No," Adele said, "It's not new, I just had it recovered. It cost almost as much as a new chair, but I love the fabric."

Fern imagined what her mother was thinking - it was a waste of money to spend so much on a chair. But the chair, the color of azaleas, was the most beautiful piece of furniture she had ever seen.

"I bought some more fabric for Fernie's graduation dress," Adele said. " This might be the last dress because once she's at college, she won't want anything I make her."

Adele discreetly handed Ann a paper bag as they stood at the door saying good-bye. Fern knew the contents of the bag would eventually appear in her closet.

Fern knew that Adele belonged to the past and her mother was a modern woman. She understood, but she wished her mother was more like Adele.

9

Ann had no time to read the newspaper, but for a whole week she looked through the papers Leo brought home. On Sunday, she eyed Fern appraisingly and said, "I think you're big enough to help. There's an ad in the paper for a sale on lamps. I'm going downtown to Gimbel's today. "

Fern was surprised and flattered - her mother never took her shopping or asked for help. On the train, she looked out the window even when it went underground. The dark tunnel walls alternated with brightly lit stations: "125th STREET, LENOX AVENUE, 57th STREET, TIMES SQUARE." Some day she would get off at each stop and look around.

In the store, swarms of women were grabbing the lamps. The best ones were gone, and they had to get something fast.

Ann held up two models, "I don't really like either, but which do you think is better?"

They made a choice and waited for the lamps to be wrapped.

"We have to hurry to get home before dark," said Ann. We don't want to stand all the way home."

On the street, people were streaming towards the subway. Fern felt she was on a mission as she walked quickly, straining to hold the bulky lamp. There were only two empty seats on the subway car, and they were far from each other.

"You take that one," Ann said when she saw Fern hesitate.

Balancing the bulky package on her lap, Fern felt strange sitting next to strangers, but she felt close to her mother at the same time. Maybe they would take more shopping trips together.

Once off the train, as they approached the entrance to their building, eager to put down the packages, a woman planted herself in front of them. She wore a rose print kerchief and small gold earrings. She smiled at Fern as if she knew her.

"You haff a beautiful girl," she said to Ann. "I vass hoping to see you. Ven vill vee get our girls together?"

Ann grimaced. "How about tomorrow, in front of the building, after school?"

"Goot, goot," the woman said, finally moving away. "Vee vill be there!"

"Who is that?" Fern asked.

"She's the mother of a girl in the next building. She's from Romania."

"Who is the girl?" Fern asked.

"Sherry."

"I don't know any Sherry," Fern said. She knew most of the girls on the block. She would have noticed a girl her age.

"Oh, sure you've seen her, she's a heavy-set girl." Heavy-set was Ann's way of saying fat. "I promised her I would introduce you. She's worried that Sherry never goes out, and she wants a friend for her."

Seeing Fern's expression, Ann added, "Look, you don't have to do anything, but at least give it a chance."

They met on the street the next day, both nervous, neither knowing what to say. Sherry had a pretty face like her mother and stood quietly in front of Fern, who didn't know what to say. What would they do? Fern never brought a friend to the apartment, and Sherry didn't ask Fern into hers.

"I have to go inside now," Fern said.

"Me too," said Sherry.

When her mother asked how it went, Fern said, "I don't like her."

"Why not?"

"I just don't."

Fern got her crayons and started to draw at the kitchen

table.Her mother had said to give it a chance, and she had. So why was she troubled?

"Fern, come here for a minute," Ann called from the living room. She stood in front of the sofa, now flanked by the lamps. "What do you think?"

"It looks nice," Fern said. The rest of the room looked shabby, but Fern didn't say that.

"I'm giving a party this weekend and I want it to look nice."

Ann cleaned and organized all week and appeared nervous that Saturday morning. "It might be a little noisy tonight but you'll fall asleep eventually. Besides, I don't do this very often,"she said.

"Who is coming?" Fern asked.

"My friends from the Satellite Social Club. Since High School, we stayed in touch even though we all live far away."

Ann wore a satiny shirtwaist dress and pearl earrings. Her dark hair was in a pixie cut, and Fern thought she looked beautiful. She would have liked to stay up to see the guests, but she contented herself with listening from bed.

The doorbell rang several times, and there were boisterous greetings. Low talk was interspersed with shouts and laughter. Fern finally drifted off to sleep, glad in the knowledge that at least her mother had friends.

＼ ＼ ＼ ＼ ＼

Sunday was raw and overcast; the stoop was deserted. Fern waited for as long as she could and then went inside.

"Nobody is out," she said.

"It's not good to stay in the house all day, I want you to go out again later," Ann said.

"It's going to rain," Fern protested.

"How about the library? As long as it's not raining yet, we can go . We'll take umbrellas just in case."

"But you told me there was no library!"

"Pelham Parkway doesn't have a library. We'll go to the Van Nest Branch. It's a long walk, but I think you're old enough."

"Why don't we have a library?" Fern asked.

"You know Arthur's mother?" Ann explained, "she's trying to get a library built."

Arthur lived in the building and Fern sometimes saw his mother, always dressed neatly with tailored suits and a briefcase. She was the only woman she had ever seen carrying one. Once Fern saw her asking people to sign a petition for the library.

"Do you think they will ever build a library ?" she asked.

"Maybe," Ann said, "it depends if they have enough money in the budget."

The Van Nest Branch was a mile away, in a neighborhood of small, neat houses. It was an old house that had been converted into a library. With its gables and bow windows, it looked like a story-book cottage.

When the librarian handed her a card, Fern asked how many books she could borrow. "As many as you want," replied the librarian.

"I mean how many can you take each time?"

The librarian smiled and assured Fern she could take as many as her arms could hold. Fern exulted: as many as you wanted, and for free!

"Would you like me to help pick out a book?" the librarian asked.

"No thank you, I want to look around."

The library was begging to be explored. Fern felt like a swimmer in unknown waters but confident in her ability.

The fairy-tale section had a colorful row of thick volumes entitled: The Red Book of Fairy-tales, The Blue, The Yellow, etc. She leafed through the Red Book, entranced by the illustrations of castles and princesses. She decided to start there and work her way through.

At home, she nestled in a living room chair and read. She could practically feel the gallop of the horses pulling the carriage, and the excitement of the peasant girl as she danced with the prince. She wondered if she would ever get to wear a ball-gown. A book was almost as good as a friend.

10

Learning came naturally to Fern. At school, her problem was shyness.

"What are the names of Christopher Columbus's three ships?" the teacher asked. Fern knew, but wasn't sure how to pronounce them, so she didn't raise her hand.

Art wasn't taught at school, but her teacher said they could draw a picture with their essay. Fern looked at the illustration in her book and drew a three-masted ship. The teacher hung hers on the bulletin board. She knew it was because most of the class didn't even do a drawing, but it still made her proud.

Not wanting to be with dullards and trouble-makers, Fern worked hard to be in the best classes, but by third grade, she felt the strain of always being good. When her teacher announced that Miss Conley, the assistant principal, needed two milk monitors, she saw a way to escape the classroom. Her hand shot up to volunteer. The smartest girls, like Kay, weren't interested - their parents didn't want them walking around the halls missing class. Fern and a girl named Deena were chosen.

Miss Conley was nice to her monitors, and Fern looked forward to Tuesday mornings. The girls went to the office, picked up lists of children with delinquent milk-money accounts, and went through the school distributing them to the teachers. Sometimes Fern took extra turns around the corridors and peeked into classrooms, but Deena hung back.

"Oh, come on," Fern said to Deena, "there's nothing to be

afraid of!" She had a feeling of importance, roaming the halls at will.

Sometimes, when they entered Miss Conley's office, they heard her scolding a child for not bringing the milk money, blaming them for their parents' oversight. One morning, as they sat in the little anteroom of the office, a moon-faced boy came in. He was around their age, and his eyes shone with defiance. Miss Conley slammed the door behind him.

"Who is that?" Fern asked Deena. "Do you know him?"

"That's Joey Roman, he was in my class last year."

They heard Miss Conley's voice, but couldn't make out the words. When the boy came out, he hesitated and turned around.

"When will I get it back?" he asked as he opened Miss Conley's door.

"Get in here!" Miss Conley roared, "and close the door." Now they could hear what she said.

"What nerve! You bring a knife to school and you want it back? This is going on your permanent record card. Now go back to class, and I better not see you here ever again."

`` ` ` ` ` ` ``

An after-school Brownie troop was forming, and Fern was excited to join. She hoped to make the ideal friend there, someone like Bess in the Nancy Drew books she was reading.

Every meeting started with the Girl Scout Pledge, promising to "do my duty to God and my country." Fern enjoyed the arts and crafts and the songs like "When E'er You Make a Promise, and Make New Friends, but Keep the Old." After a few weeks, she felt she really belonged, but there was a problem. Ann didn't think a uniform was necessary, but Mrs. Bogen, the Brownie leader insisted on it. She was taking care of their daughters; the least they could do was buy the uniform.

On a Thursday afternoon, there was an announcement over the loudspeaker for the Brownie meeting. Fern was proud to be one of girls the announcement was for, but her mood quickly changed when she entered the room.

"Where's your uniform?" the leader asked. "Didn't you remind your mother?"

When Fern told Ann about it, Ann was annoyed. " I'm not working hard to waste money on fancy uniforms. Are you sure you really like Brownies.

Fern loved being in the Brownies, but she wasn't going to endure being scolded by the leader. She decided not to go back if she didn't have a uniform. She worried about it all week.

The day before the meeting, her mother surprised her with a cleanly pressed, used uniform. As if to make up for her initial refusal, there was also a new Girl Scout Handbook.

"I wish your leader had told me you could get it second-hand. It would have saved a lot of grief," Ann said.

Over the next few months, Fern read the handbook from cover to cover; she learned about outdoor skills, knot-tying, sheep shearing, and cross-stitch embroidery. The more irrelevant the skill, the more she enjoyed reading about it.

Fern finally found the friend she was looking for. Merle was a Brownie too, and they had a lot in common. Like Fern, she lived in a three - room apartment where her parents slept on a sofabed. She had it worse than Fern in having to share a bedroom with an older sister and a younger brother.

Merle's sister was considered the smart one in the family and was going to The Bronx High School of Science. Merle thought she was as smart as her sister, but like Fern she had a problem with numbers. She said that was why her father called her "the dummy."

Both girls chafed at the school's rigid propriety. They gave each other courage for a game they called 'treasure hunt' in which they hid clues in the stairwells, the bathrooms, and even within books in the school library. The 'treasure' was a trinket or an original poem. To escape the classroom, they asked for the bathroom pass or volunteered to be a monitor. That was the hard part.

"The Brownie camp-out in June is a wonderful opportunity," Mrs. Bogen said in the middle of the year, "but you must be on your best behavior, and you have to follow all the rules."

As the day of the camp-out approached, Fern was filled with anticipation. All the girls were excited to get out of the city. Merle and some of the others had never even been out of the Bronx.

On the day of the trip, there was loud talking and shrieks of laughter as the girls boarded the tour bus. What would the food be like, and what about those bunk beds?

After the bus crossed a long bridge, Mrs. Bogen stood up in the aisle of the bus and spoke to them.

"Now that we're going to the country, it's very important that everyone stay on the grounds. It's easy to get lost. And when it's lights-out, you must stay in your cabin."

Merle had a gleam in her eye when she said to Fern, "Like I'm really gonna get lost! She treats us like babies." For the rest of the trip, they whispered about sneaking out after dark.

That night, after the twelve girls got into their bunks, Mrs. Bogen said, "It's lights-out now, just like in real Girl Scout camp. Stay in your beds unless you have to go to the bathroom." Then she added, "You're not to leave the cabin for any reason. I'll be right next door."

Ten minutes later, Fern and Merle gingerly slipped out of their bunks and started making their way to the door.

"Where are you going?" one of the girls called out. Then someone switched on the light.

'Turn it off!" Merle said in a loud whisper.

Some of the girls wanted to go along. Fern thought the plan was spoiled, but Merle said anyone who wanted could join as long as they were quiet. In the end, two other girls snuck out with them.

Fern followed Merle behind a row of deserted cabins. With darkness engulfing them, Fern realized it was a stupid idea, but it was too late.

As they approached the woods, there was a rustling sound.

"A bear!" one of the girls cried out. "It's a bear!"

They turned and ran.

Once back in the cabin, they quickly climbed into their

bunks. Moments later, Mrs. Bogen came in and turned on the light.

"I'm very disappointed in you. If this is the way you behave, there'll never be another camp-out. I'm turning the lights out now, and you better stay in the cabin."

"But there's a bear outside; what if he gets in?" Merle asked.

" There are no bears on Staten Island," the leader said.

11

Every year it got harder to find a place in Rockaway. Fern thought their bungalow that summer was cute, but Ann was worried about hurricanes.

There were many other kids in the area, and though she didn't make a special friend, Fern was content - there was always someone around.

One evening, a group of girls and boys linked arms and walked down the street singing. Fern joined them, and as they wended their way through the neighborhood, other boys and girls also joined. They formed a phalanx which people on their porches, and those on the street, stared at disapprovingly.

They sang, "Rock Around the Clock," and as they repeated the chorus, they got louder and louder.

"One, two, three o'clock, four o'clock, rock/ Five, six, seven o'clock, eight o'clock rock/ We're gonna rock around the clock tonight!"

Fern felt the excitement. There was a freedom in Rockaway that she didn't have in the Bronx.

People began to yell and shake their fists at the group. One old man said he was going to call the police. Fern wasn't sure why they felt threatened, but she didn't care. She was having too much fun.

Towards the end of summer, Fern woke up to the sound of howling winds and driving rain.

"I guess we were due for a hurricane," Ann said.

"Too bad it had to be in this shack" was Leo's response. The whole city closed down, and he was staying home from work.

The bungalow shuddered with each fierce gust, and Fern worried that the bungalow would blow down like the house in "The Wizard of Oz." Leo assured her they were safe, yet he put pillows against the windows just in case.

"What are we going to do all day?" Fern asked.

"I bought a new game called 'Scrabble," Ann said. "It's about words."

Ann explained the game, and they started to play. It was hard for Fern to make four or five letter words, so when her mother made a seven letter one and got a fifty point bonus, she was impressed.

Though at times she was scared when there was a particularly strong gust, for most of the day it was pleasant sheltering with her parents. Don was content with his clay, and Fern had them all to herself. Late in the afternoon, when Ann pointed out the quiet, Fern realized it was over.

Sunbeams peeked from the clouds, and they decided to go to the beach to see what had happened there.

Large and small branches littered the street, and at the end of the block a whole tree was down. At the beach, the ocean looked angry, and the sand was strewn with debris.Many people walked about picking things up and putting them in bags.

"I think they're Brazil nuts," Ann said. "The shell is hard, so they're probably still good to eat."

"How did they get all over the beach?" Fern asked.

"Flotsam and jetsam, what fell off ships in a storm."

They gathered as many nuts as they could carry, and when they got back, Leo used a hammer to open them. The splintered pieces weren't worth the effort.

Flotsam and jetsam were silly sounding, but Fern liked

those words. She counted the letters and saw that "flotsam" was a good Scrabble word. It had seven letters.

\ \ \ \ \

Fern worried about her mother starting work, but just as she promised, Ann was always there when Fern got home. Though busier than ever, Ann was happier. She was payroll secretary, in charge of teacher records and pay increases. The teachers appreciated her and began to include her in their monthly get togethers. It was a high point of Ann's life - she had always wanted to be a teacher. Now, she was being treated as if she were one.

Every month, they met at a teacher's house in Westchester and talked about school, their families, and their vacations. When she came home, Ann described the houses and gardens, even the furniture, but mostly she talked about the women.

Mrs. Schuman, the librarian, had hidden in the forests and fought with partisans during the war. Mrs. Barr, the art teacher, gave Ann student paintings to decorate her office, and Mary-Ann, the pretty assistant principal married a millionaire. Ann talked the most about Mary-Ann whose wedding she had attended. The young woman quit her job when she got married, but a year later, bored and lonely, she returned.

Mary-Ann wore large, colorful pieces of jewelry which Ann initially assumed were costume jewelry but later learned were real. It never ceased to astonish her that the assistant principal of a school in the South Bronx would wear diamonds and rubies to work.

Ann was usually the first one at school in the morning, and even had a key to the entrance. She needed a full night's sleep, but new tenants next door were making a racket every night. As soon as Ann got into bed, the noise began: shouting, banging, and once, even a bottle breaking. A polite note slipped under the door and then another were ignored. The racket continued.

Finally, Ann knocked on the neighbor's door one evening, but nobody answered. She was sure they were home.

Someone said it was a newlywed couple, but the Bookmans had never seen them. One day, as Ann and Fern walked through the lobby to their apartment they realized the woman in front of them was headed the same way. They saw her enter that apartment. She was dressed in black and had a long, fleshy face. She didn't look like a bride.

Fern was relieved that even ugly women could get married, but what kind of marriage was it? She had heard that a glass to a wall acts like a microphone. That night, when the noise began, she listened.

"I hope your mother puts her head in a bucket of water and drowns!" a woman's voice said. How stupid, Fern thought. It wasn't just mean. It was crazy.

After dinner that night, Ann said she had to make the noise stop. " I can't live like this, I need my sleep."

"Don't get involved," Leo cautioned. " You don't know who they are."

"What am I supposed to do? I can't take it anymore!"

"You could sleep a little later if you didn't make up the bed every morning," Leo suggested.

At that Ann became enraged. "The place would become a zoo! I'm not doing that. I'm going to make them stop. You won't have to do a thing, don't worry."

All day, Fern thought about it. What was her mother going to do? She had never thought about the sofabed. Her mother removed the bedding and folded it up every morning while she herself was still fast asleep. She couldn't remember ever seeing it open.

The next morning, Fern woke up to the sound of a loud radio.

"I'm going to put the radio against their wall every morning. Give them a taste of their own medicine," Ann said with satisfaction.

The following morning, Fern heard the radio again. That evening the bell rang. It was the newlyweds, come to complain. Ann went into the hall to speak to them. That night and for all subsequent ones, it was quiet.

"How did you make them stop?" Fern asked.

"I said I would turn off the radio if they stopped the noise."

` ` ` ` `

Ann had less time for Don. "Go out and play," she told him when he came home from school. He wouldn't go out because of Charley, a boy in the building who taunted him and took his toys. Charley's mother, one of the mahjong players, pretended not to see.

Don complained bitterly, but at first Ann didn't take it seriously. She felt sorry for the mother because she had a disabled son in an institution. The bullying continued for a few years before Ann gathered her courage to complain.

"What do you want me to do, your son is bigger than mine," Charley's mother answered. Behind her, the mahjong ladies tittered, and, red-faced, Ann retreated.

When Leo came home that night, he spoke with Ann and convinced her that Don had to fight back. He instructed Don how to gently punch Charley in the stomach.

"Don't worry, I'll be right there." Ann said, "As soon as you do it, we'll go right back into the house."

Late the next afternoon, as the women were folding their chairs, Ann nudged Don.

"Remember what Daddy said," she told him.

As soon as he gingerly punched the unsuspecting boy, Charley's mother sprang up. "Look what your son did!"

"That's right," said Ann. "Now maybe he'll stop bullying Donald!"

Fern was proud of her mother. As she went back into the building, she saw the mahjong ladies' angry looks. She restrained herself from turning around to see if anyone was following.

As soon as she entered the apartment, Ann smiled broadly. In the years to come there was no more bullying, but Ann said those years gave her ulcers.

12

There was a girl in Fern's class, a blonde in a sea of brunettes. She was ordinary in every way, but she could dance. Jenny performed at school assemblies and was popular. Fern asked her where she took dance lessons. She wanted to be her friend, but more than that, she wanted to be just like her.

Fern held her breath when she asked Ann for dance lessons. To her surprise Ann said yes. She had always wanted to be a dancer herself and was glad to give Fern the chance she never had.

Fern's excitement dulled when she saw the ballet teacher with her plain black leotard and rumpled leg warmers. And she wasn't young.

"Velcome, girls," she said with a smile. "I am Miss Natasha. Vee vill vork hard in ziss class, but you vill like it. First vee vill learn zee five positions."

During the break, one of the girls said Miss Natasha was from Russia and was a real ballerina. "On stage and everything!" the girl exclaimed. Fern was impressed.

Ballet was about music and the mirror. A woman played Chopin etudes on a piano in the corner of the studio. Mirrors lined the walls, and Fern tried to perfect her steps, all of which had French names like ronde de jambe, jete, glisse, and eleve. Not only was she learning ballet but French too.

Fern never saw Jenny because their classes met on different days, but by the time she realized it, it didn't matter. She loved ballet.

"Our teacher is from Russia," Fern told Ann.

"Ballet is very big in Russia. The greatest ballerinas are Russian," Ann said.

"Grandma's from Russia, isn't she?"

"Russia-Poland. For us, it's not the same. Even though we may have lived in Russia, we're not Russian."

` ` ` ` `

Now that she had a job, Ann decided they could afford a television. Fern was excited - everyone else already had one.

Leo waited till the weekend to set up the T.V. When he opened the box and read the instructions, Fern and Don watched eagerly.

The screen was not much larger than a notebook, but Leo said, "Stay back! You have to be at least six feet away. There's radiation that comes out. It's dangerous"

"And you're not allowed to turn it on without permission," Ann added.

No matter how Leo fiddled with the dials, all he got were black and white test patterns, so he called an electrician

By the time an electrician came and set the television up, the excitement had died, and soon they realized that instead of bringing the world into their living room, television was just an after-dinner entertainment.

Fern and Don watched Farmer Gray cartoons on Sunday mornings and the "Howdy-Doody Show." Sometimes, Fern watched "The Lone Ranger," which featured a masked man as a hero. Ann and Leo started watching the detective show, "Dragnet," which came on right after Fern went to bed.

At night, Fern lay awake for a long time - her legs ached. The first night she ignored it, but it continued for several nights and got worse. She feared she was becoming paralyzed and finally told her parents. Leo assured her it was growing pains. Two weeks later he measured her and found she had grown two inches. She was relieved when the pain finally stopped, but still she couldn't fall asleep. The insistent, sinister theme music of

"Dragnet" kept her awake, so Leo lowered the volume.

For the first time in her life, Fern started having nightmares. There was always a masked robber who sneaked in through the hall closet. That closet, which faced her bedroom door, was strange. She had always been forbidden to open it, and the few times her parents had opened it and she peeked inside, she had been surprised at the odd things she saw.

"There's nothing to be afraid of," Leo told her, but the nightmares continued, and she started waking her parents in the middle of the night out of fear.

Leo said he would open the closet for her to see for herself. Rather than pacify her though, seeing the inside of the closet increased her fear. A folded wheelchair, wooden crutches, and boxes of bandages were crammed in like pieces of a puzzle.

"You see, there's nothing to be afraid of," Leo insisted. "I't's just things for my brother Israel for when he gets out of the hospital."

The nightmares continued, and Leo suspected it had to do with television. "No more TV during the week," he said.

Fern dreaded going to bed but stopped complaining.

A short time later, Ann and Leo became bored with "Dragnet." They stopped watching the show and the nightmares ceased, never to return again.

`` ` ` ` `

On a Sunday night after supper, Fern did her math homework, and Ann looked it over.

"You got a lot wrong," she said. "You better show it to Daddy."

Leo said, "You're improving, but let's go over the ones you got wrong."

Multiplication was easy for Fern because she had a good memory, but division was hard. Every Friday there was a math test and she always studied, but that Friday, she awoke in a panic. She had forgotten to study! A light snow was beginning to fall - maybe school would be closed.

"No, they're not closing school today, it's not that bad," Ann said.

"But maybe they changed their minds. Could you turn on the radio?"

"Why are you so worried about school?"

"I forgot about the math test, and I didn't study. Please let me stay home today."

"Don't be ridiculous! Get up and get dressed. You're going to school."

"Please. You know I'm always good, and I never asked before. Last year I had perfect attendance. Just this once?"

"So the only reason you don't want to go is because of the test? Well you don't have to worry because there won't be a test today."

"How do you know?" Fern asked. Had her mother called the teacher?

"I know! That's all I can say. I promise there won't be a test."

Fern hurriedly got dressed and rushed to school. As she entered the room and took her seat, she had a flicker of doubt. Everything was as usual, and after taking attendance the teacher wrote the spelling words on the board. Should she ask? She didn't want to bring attention to the test.

When she finished copying the words, she saw written on the board, "Mathematics test postponed to Monday." Her mother was right! Now that she was a school secretary, she probably knew all about the way schools ran.

Ann could solve problems. She could sing and dance, swim, dive, paint, sew, and type. Fern was proud of her, but she wished she had the other kind of mother, the kind that was devoted to her home and arranged parties and play-dates. The kind who gave hugs and kisses.

Though Ann believed she could work full time and still do everything a good mother should, when she got home, housework consumed the rest of the day. Someday her mother would find time for her, but in the meantime Fern was glad she could take care of herself.

13

The teacher had a gruff voice. "My name is on the blackboard, but since it's so long, you can call me Mr. A," he said.
Fifth grade was going to be different - Fern's first male teacher. He looked angry, and no one had done anything yet.

Fern was sure Mr. A was an important person, not just because he was a man but because he was so big. He was the tallest man she had ever seen. Perhaps he had been a policeman and decided to become a teacher. He wore an immaculate blue suit, starched white shirt and striped tie. The tie looked as if it was choking him and making his face red. His shirt, stretched between broad shoulders, looked ready to burst. He was like a restrained bull seething with pent-up energy.

Mr. A stood by his desk with a defiant look, narrow turquoise eyes glinting. The class was transfixed. They had never seen a man like that. The men they knew were short, pale, and meek.

Mr. A warned the class to behave, but Fern wasn't listening. She was too busy studying him.

As the only man in the school, Mr. A was needed for situations that required strength, but he lacked the ability of the female teachers to maintain order with just a look.

There were 21 boys and 13 girls in the class, whereas the other classes had an even distribution. Unlike the girls, the boys couldn't sit still. As the term progressed that became a problem.

When Mr. A turned his back, a few boys in the back of the room passed around marbles and comic books. Late one afternoon, their stifled laughter interrupted his lesson. That made him furious. He strode to the back of the room, all eyes following him.

"What's going on back here? You, what's your name?" he barked.

"Fred," came a soft reply.

"Stand up! What do you have in your desk?" Something small was handed over. "Is this what you think school is for, to come here and play?"

Fred, a slight boy with strawberry blond hair, looked up and smiled thinly as Mr. A took a step closer and towered over him. "The first week of school and you're starting up already?"

When a boy was absent, Mr. A taunted him. "What's the matter with you? Just because it rained, you couldn't come to school? What are you made of, sugar?"

Fern felt sorry for red-headed Simon, pale and vulnerable - he enraged Mr. A for no apparent reason. When the class filed out of the gym after their first polio shots, little cotton balls pressed to their arms, Mr. A grabbed Simon by the collar and pulled him out of line. Simon looked ready to faint.

"What's the matter sonny-boy? Afraid of a little shot?"

"I'm glad I'm not a boy - he must hate boys," Fern whispered to Marilyn, a girl she knew from Brownies who happened to sit in front of her. Marilyn laughed in agreement.

Whenever Mr. A's attention was on the boys, Fern leaned forward and carried on whispered conversations with Marilyn. One day, she was startled to hear Mr. A say in a firm but gentle voice, "Fern, please pay attention!"

Mr. A had never reprimanded her - no teacher had. Her face burned with embarrassment. No one seemed to notice though, and soon Mr. A was back at the blackboard.

She had never broken the rules before, but now things were different. It wasn't hard following rules when there was no one to talk to. Throughout the year, she enjoyed her whispered conversations with Marilyn.

` ` ` ` `

Leo brought home the paper every day, either *The New York Post* or *The New York Times*. The headlines screamed, "Soviets Set Off Fifty Megaton Hydrogen Bomb." At dinnertime, Fern asked: "Does that mean they're going to bomb us?"

"Don't worry," Leo said, "Even if they have it, there's no way they can get it to us. They're not going to bomb us. It's what's called a 'Cold War.' There's nothing to worry about."

Fern wondered why Russia was such a terrible place.

At school they were having still another air raid drill. Usually you had to shelter under your desk with your arms over your head, but this one was out in the hall. As Fern's class filed into the hall, other classes did the same. There was absolute silence, and Fern saw many scared faces.

"Remember what I said - no leaning against the wall," Mr. A hissed.

As the time went by, it felt more like half an hour, not the ten minutes it was supposed to be. Fern saw a few boys leaning against the wall, Fred among them. He looked grim, as if standing quietly was the worst thing imaginable. Fern hoped Mr. A wouldn't notice and admitted to herself that she liked Fred. Why can't I like a well-behaved boy? she scolded herself.

"Get over here," Mr. A snarled.

Fern was relieved he didn't mean Fred.

Shamefaced, a thin, lanky boy stepped out of line. Fern looked at him sympathetically, but her attention was focused on Mr. A. whose red neck bulged from his white collar.

Most of the class thought Mr. A the worst teacher in the school, but in the middle of the year, there was a change. Ms. Wood, a serious, straight-backed, young student teacher was assigned to the class, and Mr. A toned down his behavior.

Then there was the song contest.

At the beginning of the second term, the class stared dumfounded as burly Mr. A held up a tiny, children's 45 rpm. record.

"There's going to be a song contest for the whole fifth

grade, and each class can choose a song. I brought this record for you. Let's listen and then we'll vote on it."

He put the record on a small, portable record player he had also brought. The class heard a banjo and then a singing cowboy.

"I'm a riden'Old Paint, an a leadin' Old Fran,
Good-by Little Annie, I'm off to Montan,'
Good-bye Old Paint, I'm a leavin' Cheyenne.."

"How many of you like the song?" he asked, "raise your hands." All hands shot up. "Good. I don't think it'll be hard to learn. I don't play the piano like the other teachers, so we're going to have to try a little harder."

The class was stunned. Tough Mr. A, the underdog? It wasn't just the fifth grade they were up against. He was asking for help against the whole female establishment.

"Are we going to be divided in groups?" Marilyn asked. She was wondering if she'd be in the non-singing group like she had been the year before.

"No," he said with a smile. "We're all going to sing, everyone has to pitch in."

Mr. A played the record over and over because he himself couldn't sing. He had a zeal for the project, rushing through lessons to practice.

Fern had a romantic view of cowboys. Like her classmates, she had never been west of the Hudson but loved everything about the Old West as seen on television and in the movies. The song transported her to the plains of Texas. As she sang, she imagined herself around a campfire after a round-up. The song rolled around her head all day. Who was "Old Fran" and "Old Paint?" She wasn't even sure about Cheyenne. Nobody in class 5-2 understood the song, but it didn't occur to Mr. A to explain. Still, they sang with fervor.

As Fern did her homework one night at the kitchen table, she broke into song. "I'm a riden' Old Paint, and a leadin' Old Fran," she began. Her brother and mother stood in the doorway, grinning.

"What's so funny?" she asked.

"Nothing," Ann said, stifling a laugh, "we're just surprised to hear you sing!"

"I think it's a beautiful song," Fern said.

"Too bad you sing off-key," Don mocked.

Fern never sang at home again. She appreciated Mr. A for not singling her or anyone else out for poor singing. His only criticism was that they didn't sing loud enough.

Finally, it was the day of the contest. The class was eager to perform their much rehearsed song, eager to make Mr. A proud.

The auditorium was packed, not just with students but with community leaders and officials from the district office. A hush fell over the hall as each class, in turn, took their places on the stage. The teachers, in pastel shirtwaist dresses, looked prim and professional as they seated themselves at the piano.

Fern was astounded by the melodic sweetness of the songs. Her class never had a chance! They had tried so hard, but it wasn't enough. They didn't even get an honorable mention.

The class was unusually quiet for a few days, as if chastened. Poor Mr. A! He looked downcast, but they had acquitted themselves well, and maybe that was all he had hoped for.

As the school year drew to a close, the class grew more subdued. One day, a loud knock on the classroom door made everyone start. When Mr. A opened the door, Fern saw round, dumpy Miss Doyle, the teacher in the next room. As they talked for several minutes, Fern wondered what it was about. She had never seen Mr. A in conversation with another teacher.

Returning to the class, he said, "I have to go to the office to take care of something. Miss Wood will take over, and I want you to listen to her!"

As soon as he left, Miss Wood stiffened, scared as a rabbit. She had never been alone with the class.

"Copy the spelling words from the board," she instructed.

Most of the class obeyed, but a few boys took advantage

of the situation and pulled things out of their desks. Miss Wood pretended not to notice.

Fern was finished while other students were still copying. Through the large windows, she saw huge, shifting clouds across the sky. An elephant had a long, curling trunk which turned into a giraffe's neck which then became a snake. It was like going to the zoo. If only she was allowed to draw them!

By the time Mr. A returned, the class was distracted and noisy. He disciplined the boys, but his heart wasn't in it, and Fern felt sorry for him.

14

Fern no longer stood on the stoop waiting for a friend. Now she was part of a twosome. Fern and Merle walked home from school every day and after school went skating and bike riding. They talked about school, the Brownies, and family problems. The last Brownie event of the year was going to be horseback riding, and an after school art class had just been announced. Life had never been so good.

Fern was invited to her first sleep over at Merle's, and she looked forward to it for days. However, it wasn't what she expected. Merle's mother served spaghetti from a can. Fern had never eaten anything like it- had never even tasted tomato sauce. That night, she threw up.

Merle's crowded bedroom felt strange, and Fern couldn't fall asleep. For the first time in her life she valued her own bedroom. Even though the sleep-over didn't turn out well, it seemed to cement their friendship.

After school and on weekends, they rode their bikes along the parkway, but one day they decided to go in the opposite direction, into a different neighborhood. Neat, private houses and small gardens lined the streets, and you could easily see the sky. They decided to call it "the new world."
` ` ` ` `

In April, Mr. A announced the date of the class picture.

"Make sure you wear a white shirt or blouse. If someone forgets and wears a plaid shirt, it'll spoil the picture."

Fern overheard girls talking about their poodle skirts.

When she got home, she asked if she could get new clothes for the class picture.

"Do you want new clothes or Rockaway? We can't afford both." Ann said.

Fern felt foolish for asking, and when an invitation to Marilyn's birthday party came, she didn't ask for a party dress. An outdated, tailored gray jumper from her cousin wasn't for a party, but there was nothing else.

Marilyn lived in a small, pretty brick house, the kind Fern wished she had. She was as excited to see the house as to attend the party. As soon as she walked in, she was overwhelmed by color: the table decorations, the bright felt skirts, the dresses, some plaid, some frilly pastels. Her own outfit made her feel like a tall, skinny pencil, but she still had a good time.

As Marilyn said good-bye to her guests, she invited Fern to come over after school.

"When should I come? Fern asked.

"Anytime," Marilyn said, "I'm always home."

That night at supper, Fern talked about the poodle skirts at the party, and Don asked what it was.

"It's a kind of skirt with decorations, mostly poodles. I like them but not the one Marilyn has - it looks stupid."

A loud "meow" startled her, and she saw her mother claw the air. "You sound like a fish-wife,"she said.

Don laughed.

"I am not being catty!" Fern protested. "It should be a design, but they make it look like a real dog with fur and a leash."

Fern later complained to Ann, "It's not fair! Everyone gets new clothes except me."

"Oh, stop it." Ann retorted, "You're lucky you have a cousin who gives you nice clothes."

Fern persisted. "You never buy me anything. Please, just this time for the picture?"

Ann gazed at Fern for a moment. "We'll see," she said, "I suppose you want a poodle skirt? I read those skirts are easy to make. You just cut a circle from a large piece of felt."

That buoyed Fern's spirits, but later she worried whether her mother was capable of making it. She had almost forgotten the whole incident when two weeks later Ann held up a piece of fabric and asked what she thought. It was thin white cotton with a red cherry print.

"It was only fifty cents, and I couldn't resist. What do you think?"

"It's nice," Fern answered, thinking it was for kitchen curtains or an apron.

"Oh, good, I'm glad you like it, I'm going to make a skirt for you."

"I don't think that material is for a skirt."

"Don't worry, it's going to be beautiful!"

"But you said it was going to be felt!"

"Felt is too expensive. You'll see, this will be very nice."

Fern hoped her mother would be too busy to ever make the skirt, but to her distress, the skirt was ready in time for the picture.

"Try it on," Ann said. "The waistband isn't finished, but I have a cinch belt that will hide it."

Fern put the skirt on. Her old white bucks with black replacement laces were her only shoes - they were worse than the skirt.

"It's too short, but don't worry. No one will see because you're always in the back," Ann said. Then she added, "Stop slumping, you don't want to grow up with a slouch. Stand up straight!"

`  ` `  ` `  `

Neither Merle nor Marilyn were going horseback riding. Marilyn's mother wouldn't let her, and Merle wasn't interested. Fern thought the real reason was cost. How could you not be interested in horseback riding?

Most of the mothers were going along, but Ann refused.

"You don't need me there," she said. "I have things to do at home."

"Don't you want to see me on a horse?" Fern pleaded.

"It'll have to be some other time."

A few mothers with cars drove the girls to the stable which was a few miles along the parkway from Pelham Parkway. Fern got a lift with a girl she hardly knew.

The mothers watched as the horses were brought out, and one by one their daughters were helped to mount. Fern watched eagerly, waiting for her turn. The horses didn't look like the ones in pictures - they were old and gray.

Fern winced when her horse was brought out. It was the biggest. It hung its head, and its back was covered with dark blotches.

"You got Ol' Betsy. She ain't pretty, but she's steady," the stable hand said.

They brought out a stepstool to help Fern mount and then fastened her feet in the stirrups. Once in the saddle, she looked down at the ground and it seemed far away. If she fell, it would be a long way down.

The horses kept going around the corral. Fern thought they would go on a path along the parkway where she had once seen people riding. A loud wail interrupted her thoughts.

"I don't want to!" a girl cried, as her horse stood waiting. "I changed my mind, I'm not getting on."

The girl's mother tried to calm her. "I already paid, please give it a try."

Then the stable hands tried to persuade the girl. At that moment, Ol' Betsy stopped, turned, and headed back to the barn.

Fern saw the Dutch door of the barn looming ahead, its top half closed shut. The bottom opening was only high enough for a horse to get through. There was no room for Fern.

"Hey, my horse is going back to the barn," she yelled, but nobody was looking. She wanted to get down, but her feet were stuck in the stirrups.

Fern knew she wouldn't fit under the door. No matter how low she bent her head. She was going to be beheaded! Like the queens of England.

"Help! Help me!" she screamed, but the Brownie leader

was nowhere in sight. Nor were the other mothers. The stable boys were at the far end of the corral, smoking.

When Ol' Betsy went through the opening, Fern bent her body as low as possible and squeezed her eyes shut. Her scalp stung as it scraped the bottom edge of the upper door.

Ol' Betsy went straight to her stall, to the feed bag.

Now everyone came running. The stable hands clustered around and helped Fern dismount. Once on the ground, her scalp bleeding, Fern vowed never to get on a horse again. In the office, a woman cleaned the wound, and Fern clenched her teeth. She didn't complain - she was glad to be alive.

Fern was angry all the way home. The stable-hands were teenage boys, but what about the Brownie leader and the mothers? Most of all she blamed her own mother for not being there.

15

Don's voice wavered. "Why is this night different from all other nights?" he recited in Hebrew. It was the Four Questions; they were at Grandma's for the yearly Passover seder.

Fern had memorized most of the Four Questions, but she was a girl and wouldn't be called on. She didn't really mind - she was content to watch.

The table was set with special Passover dishes and small haggadahs put out by the Maxwell House Coffee Company. The yearly seder was the only time Grandma had her daughters and their families all together. It was the highlight of her year.

Leo always brought his own family haggadah, a large old book illustrated by the artist, Saul Raskin. Fern's favorite illustration was of a huge arm parting the Red Sea. She wasn't sure what it meant. Leo explained. "It means God protected the Jewish people and it wasn't just an accident of nature," he said.

There was tension as the ceremony finished. The four cups of wine had been poured, and it was time for Elijah's cup. The angel Elijah had to symbolically enter and drink from his special glass. The problem was that instead of Elijah coming through the open door, it might be Scottie, the drunken super. Leo sprang up to close the door.

The seder felt like it went on forever, but Grandma's face shone with contentment.

When the family left, it felt strange going from a world of warmth and light to the dark streets. The train was noisy and jarring, and the floor of the subway car was littered with paper and debris. Some passengers dozed in their seats, others in drab work clothes, stared dully ahead, occasionally casting curious glances at the Bookmans. They were in a world of their own, barely aware of the surroundings.

"Do you believe in God?" Fern asked Leo. It was a question she had never asked before, but somehow it felt right to ask now. Did anyone really believe that Elijah came down from heaven to drink the wine?

Leo smiled indulgently. "You know I'm not religious, I guess I'm more of an agnostic. I believe in taking things as they are and trying to make the best of them. People who aren't sure whether or not there is a God are called agnostic. I'm a stoic, I believe in logic. Look at the facts, and use your mind, not your emotions."

"Grandma believes in God, and I think Mommy does too," Fern said.

"Whether or not you believe in God, you should always do what's right," Leo said, ending the conversation.

＼ ＼ ＼ ＼ ＼

Since school was closed that week, Ann visited Grandma the following Friday. It was a good opportunity for Fern to sleep over and go to the old shul.

"I'm glad you're going with me," Grandma told Fern. "This may be the last time I ever go. I think the shul is closing in the summer."

Fern had never seen the gray tailored skirt and jacket Grandma wore that Saturday morning.

On the street, Grandma said, "If you walk like you know where you're going, nobody will bother you."

It was a long walk, and Grandma strode so briskly that Fern had trouble keeping up. It was as if Grandma was a different person that day.

The small old synagogue was so unobtrusive that Fern would have passed it by if Grandma hadn't stopped. The words

"Adath Israel" were carved in stone over a small arched doorway. Flat stone columns flanked tall wooden doors and the brick building blended with the surrounding buildings.

Immediately inside the entrance, they went up a narrow flight of stairs leading to the women's wooden balcony. The men prayed in the main sanctuary, but the women's section was practically above the bimah, the place where the Torah was kept.

Fern looked down at the men and boys in their blue and white prayer shawls, the tallit. Sometimes they pulled them over their heads as they prayed. The Torah scrolls looked heavy, but in the middle of the service old men and even boys smaller than herself carried them around so people could touch them.

Fern was away from the main action but liked being with the women. Grandma, a rabbi's daughter, knew all the prayers, but Fern didn't know anything. She was thankful nobody noticed.

Though husbands and sons were below, the women were so absorbed in prayer, they never looked down. Men and women were separated so they wouldn't distract each other, but Fern couldn't stop peeking over the balustrade.

Grandma wore a small piece of white lace on her head, and all the women wore head coverings.

"Grandma, what about me?" Fern whispered.

"It's all right," Grandma whispered, "you're just a girl."

Fern wondered how the men and women could be so calm as they prayed and went through the rituals when the shul was about to close. They couldn't travel on Saturday. What would happen after the shul closed?

"We can say prayers and have the holidays at home," Grandma assured her. "Ours is a home religion."

The following morning, the bell rang and they assumed it was Ann though she wasn't expected that early. Grandma was surprised to see her favorite cousin Manny. They had been neighbors in Poland, but now he lived in Brooklyn, a two hour train ride away. He visited several times a year but never called beforehand.

"Manny, I'm glad to see you!," Grandma said. " I made pot roast this morning, but please, next time, call. Give me some notice."

"I don't want you should fuss, that's why I don't call," Manny said as he handed over a small package. "I know you can't get this with the butcher closed. It's flanken." Manny was a kosher butcher and always brought something special.

"Thank you." Grandma said. "Everybody's moving. I think the synagogue is closing too."

"It's also happening in Brooklyn. Jews are moving away. What are you going to do?"

" I don't go anyway," Grandma said softly, "I read my siddur at home. I don't like walking alone."

Fern had seen Manny only a few times in her life, and now she studied him. His small red face looked like it was scrubbed raw, and he wore a meticulous starched white shirt. He was a successful butcher. He seemed like such a good person, and Fern could understand how women would want to buy from him. She wished he lived in the Bronx so she could see him more often.

Grandma asked about Manny's brother in Argentina who he helped support.

"He has a hard life," Manny said. "He barely makes a living. Without me I don't know what he would do. What with Ernesto and now the twins."

"Is it that bad?" Grandma asked.

"It's very bad. They threw a rock through his store window a month ago. I had to send extra money."

"But nobody was hurt?" Grandma asked.

"It was at night just like in Germany. The Nazis! They let them in after the war, they say they let in 10,000."

There was an uneasy silence and Grandma asked, "Did he apply for a visa?"

"He applied two years ago. He's still waiting - there's a long list. I don't know if he can hold out. Business is bad. All the Jews want to leave."

Grandma brought out tea and cake and repeated the story of the mother and daughter: "When you're good, you're beautiful," she said, the words falling from her lips like a prayer.

Fern wondered if she had to be good to be beautiful or would being good make her beautiful? Most of all, she wondered what Grandma thought of her.

Alone with Ann that night, Fern asked, "What happened to my grandfather, Grandma's husband?"

"Let's sit down and we'll talk. You're old enough now." Ann began.

"It happened a long time ago. My grandfather Ferris helped my father in his store in East Harlem. They were very close, more like brothers. Ferris was an old man but came every day to help. One day when he was in the back of the store and my father was in the front, a gang came to rob the store. My father wanted to protect Ferris and he struggled with the robbers. They shot him."

Ann paused, and Fern saw her mother's large brown eyes begin to tear.

"Grandma was left alone with two children and no means of support. I had to get a job, so I dropped out of college. That changed everything."

16

The last week of school, Mr. A handed out the class pictures. Fern was afraid to look. Unexpectedly, the photographer had seated her in front. The large manila envelope sat on her desk for a few minutes before she slid the photo out. There, in the front, surrounded by new sweater sets, shiny saddle shoes, and poodle skirts, Fern's home-made skirt and scuffed bucks were on full display.

When the report cards were handed out, instead of being pleased, as she always was, Fern was shocked. Mr. A had given her a B in conduct. She had always gotten As. She thought he liked her.

At home, Ann questioned her closely. Apparently while the teacher was preoccupied with the boys, she had talked too much in class.

When Fern went to school the next day, her mother went with her. It felt strange walking to school with her mother. While she lined up in the yard as usual, Ann went straight to the assistant principal's office.

"Take out your report cards," Mr. A said as soon as the class was seated. "I'm coming around to check your parents' signatures." When he got to Fern, he asked, "What happened to yours?" "I forgot, I'll bring it tomorrow," she said.

The next morning, Fern asked Ann what Miss Conley said.

"Don't worry, I'm sure it won't happen again," Ann replied.

How could her mother know that? Wasn't she in charge of her own behavior?

"What do you mean?" Fern asked, but Ann didn't answer.

Fern was both angry and sad. She knew she hadn't been as good as she could have been, but school was over. She wouldn't have to see Mr. A again.

After Don went to bed that night, Ann sat with Fern at the kitchen table. Fern was pleasantly surprised when Ann said she had a favor to ask. Whatever it was, Fern would do it.

"You know your brother's friend Stuart, the one who had polio?" Ann said. "His mother always has Don over, and I have to reciprocate. At least once. Could you stay outside tomorrow so they can have the place to themselves?" Fern was relieved there was no mention of the report card.

The next day, Ann reminded Fern to stay outside for a long time.

"Why don't you take your skates? Just stay on the block."

Fern joined some girls jumping rope, and when they went inside, she put on her skates and went up and down the block. When she got tired, instead of going in, she remained on the stoop. She would make sure she stayed out long enough.

When Fern finally went in, she was greeted by the wide grins of the boys. They followed her into the bedroom.

Fern's underwear was draped on the dresser, over the chest of drawers, and onto the headboards, from every conceivable place in the room. The white cotton garments were old and yellowed - they looked like rags. Nobody was supposed to see your underwear! Fern was humiliated. How did they get her things? Had they gone through her drawers?

"Why did you let them?" she protested to Ann. She was furious at the boys, but blamed her mother.

"Don't take it so seriously. It was the other boy's idea," Ann said, and a moment later added, "Don't worry, it won't happen again."

For the rest of the day and the next morning, Fern avoided her mother. Her anger with the boys had gone, but for her mother it had increased. She had never given a thought to her plain, white cotton underwear, but she couldn't stop thinking about it now. Why couldn't she have something silky or with a bit of lace, and if it had to be the basic kind, why couldn't it be new and sparkling white?

"I'm sorry about what happened yesterday," Ann said later. " Let's go to the new library. This may be our last chance before we go to Rockaway, and you're allowed to keep books for the whole summer."

"It wasn't right," Fern said, and a silence hung between them. Fern would have refused if she hadn't been so eager to see the new library.

As they set out walking towards the parkway, Fern asked why they were going to cross the parkway. Ann told her the library was on the other side.

"It was supposed to be on our side, and a lot of people are angry. I'm just glad it was built."

The new Pelham Parkway library was almost as far away as the old library. Fern thought it looked like an office building. A library shouldn't look like that, she thought. It should have a cozy feel, like you were going back in time. The next time she went to the library, it would be back to the small Van Nest Branch.

She chose a book only after the librarian told her she could return it to a different library. It was a thick book so it would last a long time, and as soon as she got home she started reading."Gone With the Wind" was far better than fairytales and Nancy Drew books.

That weekend, Ann and Leo went to look at a house they saw advertised. They asked if Fern wanted to come, but she preferred to stay home. She had seen too many houses. Each one was either too small, too old, or too expensive. Once a house they had signed a contract for had fallen through. Her father insisted the house be brick in case of fire, and her mother wanted a house that was fairly new so they wouldn't have to make repairs. Fern was resigned to being in the apartment until she went to college.

"Don't stay in the house," Ann said. "It's a sunny day."

As soon as they left, Fern took her library book to the only place they wouldn't see her when they returned: the bathroom.

After closing the door, she started reading. It was quiet, and she turned the pages quickly. She was a fast reader.

She's like me, thought Fern, slim with dark hair, but she realized Scarlett's problems were far worse than hers. I can't stop liking Fred who is totally inappropriate, yet she's in love with Ashley, a married man.

A noise interrupted Fern - they had come home. Still, she couldn't put the book down. Her neck ached as she hunched over it. Did they even care where she was? After about an hour, she quietly opened the door and slipped into the bedroom.

"Oh Fern, I didn't know you were in the house," Ann exclaimed. "I assumed you were outside."

Her mother hadn't even missed her!

That night, Fern dreamt she killed her mother. The dream was so realistic that when she awoke, she looked down to see if there was blood on her hands. She didn't hate her mother! How could she when everybody loved her?

17

Every summer there were fewer places for rent in Rockaway, and an apartment in an old building close to the bay was the best the Bookmans could find. Broken down rowboats and old fishing tackle made a good breeding ground for mosquitoes. Even after Leo patched the torn screens with tape, mosquitoes plagued them all summer, but nothing could spoil the ocean.

Ann and Leo never missed a swim even when the water was frigid at the beginning of summer. Now, taller and stronger, Fern was able to handle the cold, rough water. When big waves barreled towards her, she dove under them. It made her feel brave.

When she wasn't on the beach, Fern was on the street just like in the Bronx. She immediately found a friend in Brenda, a girl down the hall. Brenda told her about the TV soap operas she watched, and in the evenings they walked around the neighborhood acting out their own stories. Fern enjoyed the roles of the jealous wife and scheming girlfriend, and the girls took turns playing the male roles which neither wanted.

One cool, cloudy day, the street was filled with children. There was the threat of rain, and no one was going to the beach.

Fern heard an older boy, Naftali, ask his friends if they wanted to go to the gym. "There's a gym?" Fern asked.

"Sure," Naftali said, "want to come?"

"Can I come too?" Brenda asked.

"Anyone who wants can come, but you have to listen to

me cause we're not really allowed."

The group followed Naftali for a few blocks to a large, old wooden building with stained glass windows.

"What is this place?" someone asked.

"It's the synagogue," Naftali said. Then he put his finger to his lips and led them down a partially hidden staircase and tried the door at the bottom. "Yup, it's open. Everybody quiet! Don't make any noise!"

They entered a large gymnasium like the one in school. "Remember we're not supposed to be here," Naftali said. Then he went to a corner and took a spalding from his pocket. Silently he and the other boys started playing ball. When the ball hit the wall, it echoed in the vast space. Fern and Brenda walked around the gym, skirting small piles of equipment.

"Don't touch anything," Naftali warned.

The small windows near the ceiling were getting dark - a storm was coming. Somewhere a door slammed and everyone froze. Then they ran.

"That's the caretaker, he chased me out last week," Naftali yelled. Fern headed to the door, but Naftali yelled, "No, this way."

Naftali led the group in the opposite direction up a staircase to the sanctuary where they hid beneath the pews. In the semi-gloom, they listened for footsteps. Fern was annoyed. He should have told them about the caretaker.

It was strange kneeling there in the huge, silent space. There were big stone tablets mounted on the wall. Fern knew what they said.

A crash of thunder interrupted her thoughts. It was so loud it felt like her head was splitting. It's the voice of God, she thought. He's punishing me! She sprang up and ran.

Everyone ran to the gym, to the exit. Standing by the door was the caretaker. He held the door open.

"That's right, run! Run away," he yelled. "But you better not come back. Next time I'll call the police!"

Fern ran as fast as she could in the pouring rain. She was exhausted but kept running. If someone asked her, she wouldn't have known exactly what she was running from.

＼ ＼ ＼ ＼ ＼

The heat of August warmed the ocean, but for city dwellers it was oppressive, especially for those without air-conditioning. Grandma was coming to stay for a few days, and Ann was glad to provide a respite.

On the beach, Fern was surprised to see Grandma remove her zippered dress to reveal a long-skirted bathing suit.

"Does Grandma swim?" she whispered to Ann.

"No, but she loves the water. She jumps the waves."

Grandma joined a few elderly women who clutched an underwater rope running along the jetty. When a big wave came, they jumped with excitement.

A few days later, when Grandma was getting ready to leave, she asked Fern if she'd like to go back with her and sleep over. Fern wanted to, but Ann wasn't sure.

"Why do you want to go?" she asked. "It's going to be very hot. What will you do there?"

"If she wants to sleep over, it'll be no trouble," Grandma assured Ann. "I'll be glad of the company."

Ann agreed reluctantly. "I guess it's all right. Leo can pick her up after work."

When she said good-bye, Fern got the feeling her mother was disappointed. Couldn't she understand she just wanted to spend time with Grandma? It wasn't as if she was choosing the Bronx over Rockaway.

They left in the morning before the heat of the day, but by the time they got to Grandma's there were heat waves rising from the pavement.

Once inside, Grandma turned on a big floor fan and a window fan, and pulled down the shades. It didn't make the apartment cool, merely bearable.

After having something to eat, Grandma sat next to the radio and motioned for Fern to join her.

"Be quiet. This is my favorite program," she said.

A man's deep voice intoned:

"This is The Romance of Helen Trent, the real-life drama of a woman who fights back bravely to prove that because a woman is thirty five or more, romance need not be over. . ."

Grandma listened to the program every day, and she explained the story to Fern during the station breaks. Helen loved Gil, but her former boyfriend, Brett, refused to give her up. She tells him she just wants to be friends, but Brett gets angry and says that a man and woman can never just be friends.

Fern wondered why her grandmother listened to such a program. What did she have in common with Helen Trent? She was Grandma who cooked and cleaned and made the holidays for her family. What did she know about boyfriends?

18

All summer Fern looked forward to having Mrs. Corelli for sixth grade, the most popular teacher in the school. When the class was told she was on sabbatical in Italy, they groaned in disappointment. Her replacement, Mrs. Wakefield, said Mrs. Corelli would send them each a postcard from different places in Italy, and that made them feel better.

There were other disappointments for Fern. She was seated next to Albert, a boy she didn't know, and for the first time she was in the front of the room. She could no longer look around at her classmates or out the window. When she thought about it, she realized her mother must have requested it.

Something else was different: the new desks were actually tables shared by two students. For children with little private space at home, having one's own desk was important.

A loud thud from the back of the room was followed by a boy's angry voice, "He put his books on my side!"

"That's no excuse for knocking them down," the teacher said.

The two boys glared at each other.

"If your books end up on my side, don't worry," Albert said to Fern in a whisper. "It won't bother me."

To Fern's relief, Albert was a very agreeable boy, and they quickly became friends. He even gave her a nickname, "Sexy Sue." Like most of the other girls in the class, she hadn't yet started developing. How could he see her, so thin and gawky as sexy? She liked the nickname though.

She started to notice him in the morning on her way to school. He came with his mother and her miniature French poodle. His mother's tight curls and high heels matched the dog. So did short, sweet Albert.

` ` ` ` `

"I'd like to see her four carat ring," Fern said to Ann as they walked to Adele's house on the Jewish holidays.

Ann laughed. "So would everybody! She mentions it a lot, but no one remembers ever seeing it. I think she keeps it in a safe deposit box."

"What's the purpose if you never wear it?"

"In Europe, Jews were sometimes able to escape the Nazis by selling their jewelry. Maybe it gives Adele a feeling of security."

As soon as they arrived, Fern checked for the ring and was disappointed. As her parents chatted with Adele, she took her usual place at the piano. Too soon her parents arose from the sofa, signaling it was time to leave. She would have liked to stay longer - just being in those opulent surroundings was a treat.

As they said their good-byes, the door opened and Big Fern came in. Adele asked them to stay a bit longer, but before they even had a chance to reclaim their seats, Big Fern, heading towards the bedroom said excitedly, "I have to get ready, my boyfriend is coming over."

A moment later she emerged from the bedroom, her long hair gleaming. She was wearing a beige tailored sheath that fit perfectly. Fern hoped someday she too would wear such a dress. Did her cousin even appreciate Adele's handiwork?

"Mom, can I talk to you?" Big Fern said, taking Adele aside.

A minute later, a flustered Adele turned to Ann and Leo and told them they had to leave immediately. "I'm sorry, Fernie doesn't want it to look like she invited the whole family over to inspect her boyfriend."

Leo's mouth was a thin tight line as he arose from the sofa.

Then the doorbell rang.

"Quick!" Big Fern said. "That's him! Get into the bedroom and close the door. Don't come out till he's gone. And be quiet!"

The Bookmans filed into the bedroom and closed the door. As the minutes ticked by, Fern wondered if they were allowed to leave to use the bathroom. She felt sorry for her parents.

When Adele finally opened the door, the couple was gone. Apologetically, she explained she was hoping they would soon be engaged. Again, as the Bookmans were about to leave, she stopped them. "Wait, I almost forgot," she said, thrusting a large paper bag into Ann's arms.

"I don't care what's in the bag, I'm not wearing it," Fern declared when they got to the street.

"We have to appreciate what we have," Ann said sharply.

Leo was silent and stony-faced the whole way home.

` ` ` ` `

Because her birthday came around the start of the school year, birthday presents were always school supplies. Birthdays in the family were simple affairs, as if to say: "You're a year older, but let's not make a big deal of it." Fern hated that.

Ann's own birthdays, when she was young, had always been in the street. Grandma told Fern she always made two cakes, one chocolate, one vanilla, and put them on a table in front of the store. Then she would call out to the neighborhood children.

Fern looked forward to getting her grandmother's birthday cards which always arrived precisely on the day of her birthday. Grandma never forgot. Old-fashioned flowers and bows in pastel colors decorated the cards, and sweet hand-written messages were inside. Grandma must have a box filled with cards like that, Fern guessed.

On the night of her birthday, Leo brought home a large box of chocolate eclairs from Snowflake Bakery. After the family sang Happy Birthday, Ann took out the presents. Fern opened a little box from her mother which she hoped was the scatter pins that everyone was wearing. She was disappointed that it was a green neckerchief for assembly.

"The old one was frayed," Ann explained.

Fern was sure the large box would have something better, and it did. She was grateful to her mother as she lifted out a turquoise felt skirt decorated with sombreros and serapes. Then she read the card: "Happy Birthday, from Aunt Adele."

` ` ` ` `

Fern was usually nervous speaking in class, but her new skirt gave her confidence. The class was doing a unit on geography, and she had chosen Mexico for her report. She recited her own poem for extra credit.

"To Mexico we shall go/ A land of no winter or snow,
What glorious fun/ We'll play in the sun,
And remember long after/ The whole trip is done."

"That was excellent," Mrs. Wakefield said. "Maybe other students who haven't gone yet can write a poem about their countries."

The class didn't look happy - a few boys glared at Fern. On the other hand, Albert beamed - he was proud of her, as if she belonged to him.

Fern and Albert generally agreed on things, and at their table they talked whenever they could. When they weren't at their desk, things were different. She was embarrassed to be a head taller, and he seemed to like her more than she did him. In any event, true friendship with him was impossible - he was a boy.

Albert surprised Fern when he nominated her for class secretary. She thought no one would vote for her, but she won, and for the first time felt popular.

Kay, the teacher's pet, was elected vice-president. She sat in the front of the room and never took her eyes off the teacher. She didn't talk except to answer the teacher's questions. Kay's friend Pamela was the school celebrity. Because she was on "The Children's Hour," a popular television program she only went to school four days a week. While the teachers were in awe of her, the students resented having to sit through her piano recitals at assembly. Neither ever smiled or spoke to Fern. They were rich girls with stylish clothes, professional hair-do's, hovering parents, and birthday parties to which she was never invited. At times Fern felt left out, but now that she had a best friend, it didn't matter so much.

〟 〟 〟 〟 〟

It was only at Brownie meetings that Fern saw Marilyn anymore, and she missed her. Since Marilyn had said she was always home, Fern decided to visit. Her walk from Netherland Avenue took ten minutes, but she almost turned back more than once. She wasn't sure if Marilyn would be glad to see her.

At the front door, she hesitated. She assumed Marilyn would come to the door, but it was Marilyn's mother instead.

"Marilyn's upstairs," she said curtly, and Fern felt the woman's eyes on her as she walked up the stairs. It was a relief when Marilyn greeted her warmly.

"Oh it's Fern!" Marilyn exclaimed delightedly as Fern entered the room. The pink and white room looked like picture from Life Magazine.

Two girls were sprawled on a white shag rug, reading magazines. One of them looked up. "I'm Millie, I live next door, and that's Ellen."

"What happened with the horseback riding?" Marilyn asked.

Fern told them about her adventure with Ol' Betsy, and the girls laughed. For the first time Fern saw the humor in it.

"Nobody liked it." Marilyn said "A lot of girls told me their legs were sore for a week."

The girls got back to their magazines, and Marilyn held out a "True Romance" to Fern. Ann wouldn't approve, but she would never know. Fern flipped through and read "He Left me for My Best Friend, A Shocking Story of Betrayal." She loved it.

"Are you finished already?" Marilyn exclaimed, looking up from her own story.

Fern looked around the room again. It was very large and

had lots of furniture. So much for just one girl!

When the girls finished reading, they talked about the Jewish holidays.

"Is your family going to the Jewish Center?" Millie asked Marilyn.

"I'm not sure where we'll go," Marilyn said. "My father joined three synagogues."

"Why did he do that?"

Marilyn laughed. "The first because he likes it, then the J.C.C. because my brother goes to Hebrew school there, and Young Israel because it's the only one with air-conditioning."

Fern hoped no one would ask where she was going - she wasn't going anywhere. Her parents weren't members of any synagogue. They only went to the free memorial service at the J.C.C. on Yom Kippur, the Day of Atonement.

19

Fern and Don sat at the kitchen table, their school books spread before them. When Don pointed to a word and asked what it meant, Ann put down the dish she was drying and peered over his shoulder.

"I'm not sure," she said. "We better ask Daddy, he's better at Hebrew."

When Leo saw Don's problem, he was annoyed. "That's aleph, the first letter of the alphabet. Why don't you know it?"

Leo opened the Hebrew book to the first page, and said, "Here's the alphabet, let's go over it."

Now it was Don's turn to be annoyed. He started reading, then complained that he knew it already.

Fern looked at the Hebrew letters - they were like teardrops and musical notes.

"How come Don goes to Hebrew school and not me?" she asked.

"You can go instead of me." Don said. "But why would you want to?"

"Aren't there any girls in your class?"

"Only the rabbi's daughter."

"It's not fair!"

Ann explained, "Boys have to go for their bar mitzvahs, and girls don't."

Fern was annoyed. A minute later, she turned to her father. "Why don't we ever go to synagogue?"

"We are going," he said. "We joined the J.C.C."

Fern was happy to hear that, even though she was sure it was mainly for Don's bar mitzvah preparations.

A week later, Fern proudly walked through the great synagogue doors. She wore a light blue coat with a navy velvet collar that Ann had bought for the occasion. She looked around the crowded pews. Marilyn was not there - she had probably gone to one of the other synagogues.

The congregation stood and started chanting:

"Adonai, melech, Adonai maloch, Adonai y'imloch, l'olam va'ed."

The blended voices seemed to come from the building itself. Her father knew the words, but she didn't. Fern asked what it meant.

"Our lord is the ruler; He has been and will be in this world and beyond," Leo translated. He explained that there were many names for God, but the true name could never be known and never be spoken.

For a long time Fern heard the chanting in her head. It always comforted her.

＼ ＼ ＼ ＼ ＼

At the after-school art class, one girl's work stood out. Fern had never seen student art work that good. Estelle, the artist, was the girl who had once come into her fifth grade class to talk to Mr. A. With her chopped off hair and ragged skirt, she looked like a refugee. After talking to Mr. A for a few minutes she had left, and Fern hadn't seen her again until the art class.

As the term progressed, they sat together and became friends. Estelle no longer looked bedraggled. She had long, shiny black hair and almond-shaped eyes. She was beautiful. Having just arrived from Italy, her teacher had sent her to Mr. A because he supposedly spoke Italian. It turned out all he could say was "Bongiorno."

One day, after Fern complimented her drawings, Estelle said they were nothing compared to the paintings she had at home. She asked Fern if she'd like to see them and invited her over after school.

Estelle's building was similar to Fern's, as was her apartment. They went straight to the bedroom which had two single beds. Fern thought it odd for a mother and child to share a room. The walls were completely covered with paintings of underwater scenes, interiors, deserts, and jungles, all painstakingly drawn and painted with bright, unusual colors. She is a good artist, Fern thought, much better than me.

Estelle told Fern she had been born in Palermo, a city in southern Italy. She and her mother had travelled throughout Europe after her father died in the war. She went to the original Montessori school in Rome and to a children's art school in Paris.

The apartment had three rooms, and was even smaller and darker than Fern's. As they went to the kitchen for a drink, in the gloom of the living room, Fern noticed two old people on the couch.

"Who are they?" she whispered.

"Oh, ignore them, they're just my grandparents," Estelle said.

Fern asked where they slept, and Estelle said the living room. "Did they come here after the war?" Fern asked, assuming the apartment was Estelle's mother's.

"No, they've been here a long time," Estelle explained. "It's their apartment. We're only staying till we get our own place in Manhattan. I can't wait. I hate it here."

As Fern was leaving, Estelle grabbed her jacket and said she would walk her home. Fern noticed she didn't say good-bye to her grandparents.

A few days later, Estelle called Fern and asked if she would like to sign up for art lessons at the 92nd street Y. Fern was grateful that Ann agreed. Going to the class with Estelle on Sunday mornings became the highpoint of Fern's life.

The teacher was a young, attractive woman who told the girls (there were no boys) to just call her Felicia. She had studied with the famous artist Hans Hoffman, whose theories about art were the basis of the class. Felicia patiently explained that there was a dynamic force operating on every artist's canvas called the "push and pull" effect. It was hard to understand, but the class was impressed.

Most of the time they drew still lifes with pencil and charcoal. Some in the class had an innate ability to draw, but Fern found it challenging. She concentrated hard but was frustrated by having to repeatedly draw arrangements of boxes and bottles. Felicia said they would have live models only when they were ready, probably the following term.

One day, a classmate asked Fern why she didn't have a portfolio. Fern had been rolling up her drawings to bring home. "You'll need a portfolio to get into the High School of Music and Art," the girl said.

Estelle told Fern that she was planning to go to the High School of Music and Art, and one of the reasons she was taking the class was to build up a portfolio. Fern wasn't sure if she wanted to go too but figured she might as well build a portfolio .

Towards the end of the term, the class was assigned an exciting scene using tempera paint. Fern chose to do a three masted ship tossed by the waves. As she painted, she could practically feel the ship sway. The painting wasn't as detailed as Estelle's, but its roughness gave it a wild feeling. It would be the first thing to go in the portfolio - the portfolio she didn't yet have. She longed for the black leatherette type some of her classmates had. There were other art supplies she needed too, but remembering the unpleasantness with the Brownie uniform, she hesitated to ask. When she finally did, Ann surprised her.

"Get whatever supplies you need, and get yourself a nice portfolio," she said, handing Fern four dollars.

Fern went to the art supply store with anticipation, but the portfolio alone cost twelve dollars. She got a thin, oaktag model for $2.50 - all she could afford after buying pencils, charcoal, and kneaded erasers. Fern didn't blame her mother. How could anyone know the high cost of art supplies?

20

Even though she wasn't the best in her ballet class, Fern was assigned the lead in the school recital. She wondered if it was because she was the tallest and thinnest. Nevertheless, she enjoyed wearing a new pink leotard and being the center of attention. At the recital, she overheard a woman next to her mother say in a loud whisper, "Look at that girl. She's so thin, you can see her ribs."

Fern couldn't understand how people got fat - it was an ordeal just getting through dinnertime. To hear her mother say apologetically, "Tonight we're having a vegetarian meal," made Fern happy. Anything was better than fried smelts or what her mother called "Salisbury Steak," which was actually a hamburger.

A week after the recital, Ann took Fern to the doctor and told him she was worried about her thinness. The doctor assured Ann there was nothing wrong, but Ann wasn't through.

"Doctor, please look at her back. I think something might be the matter with it."

Fern flinched. She thought this was a routine check-up. Why hadn't her mother told her the real reason?

"There's nothing wrong with her back," the doctor said, "but a brace might help her posture."

"I don't want a brace!" Fern protested, and she continued to object on the way home.

Ann didn't mention the brace when they got home, but that evening she told Fern she would take her to the ballet to see Maria Tallchief, the first American Indian ballerina. Fern couldn't stop thinking about it, and there was no more talk about the brace for the next few weeks.

At the City Center Theatre, they sat high in the balcony, and Ann read the playbill to Fern. "The Firebird" was a ballet made specifically for Maria Tallchief whose father was an Osage Indian.

In her bright red costume, Tallchief was like a bolt of lightning on the dark stage. When she jumped, it looked like she was flying. If an Indian could be a star ballerina, maybe a girl from the Bronx could too.

As Fern got ready for bed that night, she arched her foot and imagined wearing real ballet shoes.

"You don't want to continue with ballet and go on toe, do you?" Ann asked.

"Ballet shoes look very uncomfortable," Fern said.

"Let me see your foot," Ann said, taking Fern's foot in her hand.

"You don't really want to be a ballet dancer, do you?"

"Why are you asking? Are you going to stop my lessons?"

"No. I didn't mean that," Ann said. "It's just that your feet are like Daddy's. Flat as a pancake."

The brace was delivered a few weeks later, and Fern was horrified. It looked like a corset with bands and straps. Ann coaxed her to try it on, saying it was already paid for. It took a long time to adjust, and it pressed on her shoulders and imprisoned her chest.

"I'm not wearing it," Fern said.

"No one will see." Ann coaxed. "I know it feels uncomfortable, but you'll get used to it."

As Fern put her clothes back on, she was overcome with longing for new clothes - for something nice to cover her body.

\ \ \ \ \

The following morning, Ann asked Fern if she'd like a malted after school. What was the occasion? Sometimes her mother gave her two cents for a pretzel on her way home from school, or ten cents for an egg-cream, but never an expensive malted. Her mother surprised her even more by saying she could have a malted every Friday for the rest of the year.

"It'll put some weight on you. The doctor said to fatten you up."

"Thanks, Mommy," Fern said. "Fridays are going to be my favorite day."

On Friday she thought about the malted all day. When she was finally seated at the candy store counter, she watched every move of the soda jerk as he made her drink. First came a squirt of U-Bet chocolate syrup into a tall, metal beaker, then a scoop of vanilla ice cream, malt, milk and carbonated water. It all went into the mixer and was poured into a tall glass. There was always some left in the beaker. That became a problem.

"Did they give you the whole malted?" Ann asked a few weeks later. Seeing a quizzical look on Fern's face, she continued, "There's usually some left over. You're entitled to that."

Fern was surprised - she had never gotten what was left over.

"I didn't know you were supposed to get it," she confessed.

"You're paying for it!" Ann said sharply.

The next time Fern went for the malted, she was nervous. She didn't want to ask the unfriendly teen-age boy for a refill. She entered the store with trepidation and watched carefully as he made the malted. When she finished, she saw the boy in the front of the store with a group of children, darting around giving out candy and making change. He must have forgotten she thought, but what would she tell her mother?

The following Friday, Ann reminded her to get the refill as if she had gotten it the week before.

Today, I'll say something, Fern silently vowed.

After school, she lingered to watch a group of boys in the schoolyard - she was in no hurry.

When she entered the candy store, it was dark and empty. Where were all the kids? Even the soda boy wasn't there. She took her usual seat at the counter. The only sound was from the large ceiling fans slowly turning. From behind the counter, a man she had not seen before came towards her. Fern thought he might be the owner.

She ordered the malted as usual and watched him go through the familiar steps. He wore a long white apron and his shirt-sleeves were rolled up. As he poured the malted, Fern saw the tattooed numbers on his arm. She didn't want the rest of the malted but took a last sip with a loud sucking sound. Before she could ask, the man was in front of her pouring it into her glass. Her eyes again went to the tatoo. He set down the beaker and rolled down his sleeve.

Fern was relieved but disturbed. The man had been in a concentration camp. Her parents had told her very little about it, and this was the first time she had seen the numbers tattooed on someone's arm.

That night, alone with her mother in the kitchen, Fern asked about it. Ann said they should sit down - she would try to explain.

"I guess you must have seen something," Ann said. "There are some people in the neighborhood who were in concentration camps, but they usually wear long sleeves. They're not ashamed. It's just that the things the Nazis did were so horrible, they just want to forget. Nobody wants to talk about it. Your uncle Sol was in a concentration camp. He was one of the lucky ones who got out because it was at the end of the war."

"You never told me," Fern said.

The next week, when Ann gave her malted money, Fern said she didn't need it; she didn't like malteds anymore.

21

Every spring, Ann and Leo searched for a house, but Fern no longer went along, or even had much interest. She was sure they'd never get a house. Then one evening she overheard her mother say to her father, "There's a complete apartment in the basement that could help pay the mortgage."

The next day Ann explained the situation. "It's funny how we've been looking for a house for so long and yesterday at the dentist, a house came to us. I overheard him saying to a patient, 'Good luck with selling your house.' He told me a widow whose children were grown was selling her house, and its just what we're looking for. It even has an apartment that Sol could move into."

Sol was Leo's half-brother whom Fern hardly knew. She had only seen him at weddings and family occasions. He was a bachelor twenty years older than Leo.

Ann later spoke to the widow, and they agreed on the terms. They were both grateful to avoid a broker's fee.

"When can I see it?" Fern asked.

"We're going to wait until it's all settled. We can't get our hopes up."

"What do you mean?"

"We have to sign a contract, and until that's done we can't be totally sure."

A few weeks later, Ann explained that there was a problem. The woman loved the garden and especially the roses she had planted. They would be in full bloom during the summer.

She couldn't bear to leave her American Beauties, Lady Doncasters, and magnificent Peace Roses.

"She is a lonely woman," Ann said. "The roses are like her children."

Fern was sure the house would be another disappointment, but a week later, Ann told her she had gotten the woman to sign.

"I agreed to let her stay until the end of summer though I wanted to spend the summer in the house. I promised she could visit anytime and cut as many roses as she wanted.

Fern was stunned - she would finally get her own room!

\ \ \ \ \

During the school year, students brought in postcards from Rome, Florence, Venice, and villages throughout Italy. Mrs. Wakefield used a pointer to show each place on the map. Fern was eager for her own card, but more than half the year was over, and it still hadn't come.

"I think Mrs. Corelli forgot me," she complained.

"Don't be silly," Ann said. "The year isn't over yet."

" I'm always waiting for something that never comes!"

"All things come to he who waits," Ann said with a smile. "Now that we bought a house, you can get a dog. It has to be a small black one with smooth fur so it'll be easy to take care of. And a male."

Fern had just turned twelve - to get a dog at the ASPCA, she only needed a letter from her mother. She had long given up hope for a dog; now the problem would be finding the right one.

Fern felt grown-up as she and Don took the train into Manhattan. She had never taken Don on the train before, but he was no trouble and looked out the window the whole way.

There were aisles and aisles of dogs at the shelter but very few puppies. When she finally saw one that fit her mother's requirements, she was amazed. She cuddled the small black puppy and immediately named him "Shadow."

Shadow had to be examined before he was adopted, and

the veterinarian was on his lunch break. Fern persuaded the receptionist to allow her to take the puppy for that hour to a nearby park. She watched him toddle on his little legs, and when she picked him up he licked her face.

An hour later, Fern's happiness turned to despair when the veterinarian said, " This dog is blind."

"But he was playing like a normal dog. Are you sure?" Fern pleaded. The veterinarian said he was sure, but Fern asked, "Can't we still have him? We'll train him so he won't need to see. He can use his sense of smell and hearing."

"I'm sorry," the veterinarian said. "It's not allowed."

There must be ways to train a blind dog - Fern was sure of it. But who would listen, who even cared? The trip home was the saddest of her life.

"Isn't there something we can do?" she asked Ann.

Ann sighed. "A lot of dogs have to be put to sleep. Some of them have nothing wrong with them. It's just that nobody wants them. Maybe later on you can go back for another one."

"No, I'm not going back. I don't even want a dog any- more," Fern sobbed.

`  ` `  ` `

The following Sunday, Ann made a picnic. Even though the lawn on the parkway was only steps away, Fern was excited. Everyone was glad to get out of the apartment.

Flowering crabapple trees softened the lines of the parkway, and once they settled onto a grassy spot beneath a tall oak, it was almost like being in the country.

They sat on an old quilt and ate cheese sandwiches. The bread was soggy and the cheese tasteless. Fern took tiny bites, hoping her mother didn't notice her hand stealing into the gar- bage bag.

"Why do we always eat cheese?" she asked.

"Because Daddy and I have ulcers. We can only eat bland food."

"Is that why you like cottage cheese so much?"

"We don't like it that much, but it's good for the stomach."

On the way home, they passed benches crowded with old people basking in the sun. Pigeons milled at their feet, and in their grey and brown sweaters, the people themselves looked like large birds. I will never be like that, Fern thought - sitting on a park bench, doing nothing!

After school, the next day, Ann told Fern she had to talk to her. "It's about Daddy. Don't be upset. He's all right now, but he had to go to the hospital because of his ulcers. He's not coming home tonight, but he will be home in a few days when he's all better."

"I don't understand," Fern said, "you told me as long as you eat right, everything is okay."

"There are other things. Aggravation can cause ulcers. We have to be careful not to aggravate Daddy."

After dinner the phone rang, and Fern overheard her mother say, "Bleeding ulcers."

When Fern came home from school the next day, Ann said, "I'm going to the hospital to visit Daddy. You'll have to watch Don. I'll be home before eight."

That night Fern watched the clock. As the hand approached seven-thirty, she began to worry. It was bad enough her father was sick, but what about her mother? The subways were dangerous at night.

Finally, a little after eight, Ann came home, breathless. "Everything is all right," she reassured Fern. "Daddy is much better and he'll be home Friday."

Leo returned to work, and everything seemed fine, but a few weeks later, the pain began again. He went to one doctor after another, but nothing helped. They all gave him pills for his ulcers. One day, when Fern came home from school, Ann said that he was back in the hospital.

"It's a good thing he went to a new doctor on our health plan. He left work because of the pain and the doctor rushed him to the hospital - his appendix was about to burst. That doctor saved his life!"

A week later, Leo came home looking thin and haggard.

He got into the habit of going straight to bed when he came home from work, getting up only for supper.

22

The Bookmans had to make other plans for the summer. Urban renewal had begun in Rockaway; the old bungalows and large, frame houses were being torn down to make way for low-income housing projects.

Ann asked Fern if she wanted to go to sleep-away camp, but Fern had heard girls at Brownies talk about bad food, cold bunks, and mean counselors. "I never want to go to camp," she said.

Ann decided to try the country. She had seen an ad for Lyle Lake Bungalows which wasn't too far from the city. Leo could come up for weekends and take his three week vacation there. They decided to see it that weekend.

Fern was glad to get out of the city. She was eager to see the place where she'd be staying for the summer.

They took the El to Forty-Second street where they boarded the New York Central train. An hour and a half later , they got off the train and took a taxi to Yorktown Heights.

A pretty arbor framed the entrance to the bungalow colony; a path led to a small bungalow with a sign that said "Office." As soon as they entered, the owner rose from his desk to greet them.

"Would you like a drink?" he said, "soda or iced water?"

"A glass of water would be good," Leo said.

"We have the purest water here," the man said, as he handed the glass to Leo. "Wait till you see the lake. It's very pure; there are a lot of fish. That's how you know its clean."

"We came for the lake," Ann said, "we love to swim."

"I have just the cabin for you, right by the lake."

The large lake was surrounded by dense woods, and the cabin was steps away, but when Ann heard the price, she asked if there was something less expensive. In the end, they settled on another cabin farther from the lake.

As they waited at the entrance for the taxi to pick them up, Fern walked around, exploring. Once in the cab, she told her parents she had seen a broken wooden sign in the bushes that said, "Whites Only."

"Oh, that was an old sign, I'm sure it doesn't mean anything," Leo said.

Ann didn't say anything, but Fern saw her frown.

That week, Fern finally got her postcard from Mrs. Corelli. It showed a mountainous, flower covered island in a turquoise sea - the Isle of Capri. It was the most beautiful post-card anyone had gotten. Fern wasn't even sure the picture was real. Someday she would see for herself.

The class wasn't that interested in her post-card. Now they had more important things to think about. Their time at P.S.303 was almost over. Most would be going to the local junior high, but those who scored high on the "S.P." test would complete three years in two at a different school. "S.P." meant special progress; it was only for the top 10% of the students. On the last day of school, the results of the S.P. test would be revealed.

There were other exciting things that week like the graduation brochures that Mrs. Wakefield handed out.

"You have a week to place your order. Take these home and decide what you want," she said.

The class broke into excited chatter, especially about the autograph albums.

"Are you getting real leather?" one student asked. "What about the one with the lock and key?" and, "Which color do you like?" said others.

Fern slipped the brochure into her notebook. Her mother wouldn't give her money for something as frivolous as an autograph album. That night she asked anyway. When she saw the look on her mother's face, she added, "Everyone is getting one."

"If everyone jumped off the Brooklyn Bridge, does it mean you should too?" was Ann's response.

Since third grade, Fern had been putting money into a student savings account. She asked if she could use that money for the album, but Ann said she better save it for next year's school supplies.

"I don't think that's fair," Fern muttered.

For the rest of the week, when Fern overheard talk about the albums, she consoled herself with the thought of Lyle Lake. To swim in a lake surrounded by trees would be wonderful, but on Saturday, her expectations were crushed. Ann told her they weren't going.

"It's just not for us," Ann said.

That night, Fern overheard her parents talking. The owner had sent back the deposit with a flimsy excuse.

"Anti-Semite," Leo said. So that was it! That was why she would never swim in Lyle Lake.

＼ ＼ ＼ ＼ ＼

On a sunny afternoon, Fern and Merle rode their bikes to the "new world." They stopped in front of a big, brick house. A rose-covered arbor framed the entrance, and a large tree grew in front. I will never live in such a house, Fern thought. Next door was a small plain house that Fern could imagine herself in, and next to that a smaller one. "I'd even take that" she told herself. She wasn't sure who she was bargaining with. She'd settle for anything to have her own room.

Fern had never seen the inside of the house they were buying; she wouldn't allow herself to be happy. She hadn't seen it because Ann didn't want to disturb the seller. Ann explained she would be unsure about the house until the day they moved in.

＼ ＼ ＼ ＼ ＼

When she saw the small box on the kitchen table three weeks later, Fern wasn't thinking about the autograph album, but when Ann said, "It's for you," she guessed right away. The surprise was that it was the deluxe model engraved with her initials, and with a lock and key. It was also blue, her favorite color.

"How did you know exactly what I wanted?" Fern asked.

Ann smiled and told Fern to eat her breakfast so as not to be late for school. "There isn't time now, but I wrote something in it for you. Read it when you get to school."

Fern went around collecting autographs that day and every other day until the end of school. She treasured all the autographs, but it was her mother's that she valued most:

"This above all, to thine own self be true." Daunting advice for a girl who, for seven year had been taught to obey.

Her classmates wrote silly things like: "First comes love, then comes marriage/ Then comes Fern with a baby carriage."

Her teachers wished her "Good luck" in cursive script so perfect it could have come from a penmanship book. Even Mr. A wrote beautifully, and his brief message meant more to her than all the others.

`  ` ` ` `

On the last day of school, Fern eagerly looked at her report card. Her assignment for junior high was 7SP2, Art and Literature Class. She had made the S.P.s!

Sixth grade at P.S. 303 had been her best year: a good teacher, a best friend, class secretary, a new house, a post-card from the most beautiful place on earth, the autograph album, and now a special program for art and literature. Life had never been better!

At three o'clock, as all the students left, Fern and Merle sat on a bench in front of the principal's office and exchanged autograph books. Each carefully copied a poem they had written together. The last line was, "We will be friends until the world ends." As they wrote, a crowd of mothers came storming down the hall towards the principal's office.

"My son didn't make the S.P.s and Joey did?"

"My boy is just as smart!"

"So is my daughter!"

"Mine too!"

As they walked home, Merle poured her heart out. She had been sure she would make the SPs like her older sister. She couldn't accept that she hadn't made it.

"What will I tell my mother? Now my father will say I'm a dummy!"

When they reached the corner, Fern said, "I guess we won't be going to school together next year."

"You mean you made the S.P.s?"

Fern thought Merle already knew.

"You probably think you're an elite now!" Merle spat out.

They were already at the corner where they always parted. Merle turned quickly and walked away.

I didn't even have a chance to say I was sorry she didn't make it, Fern thought. She acts as if it was my fault!

Over the next two weeks, Fern hoped for a call from Merle but none came. Once, when they passed on the street, they avoided each other. They had walked home from school almost every day for four years, had ridden bikes together, shared secrets, and pledged to be friends for life. Merle had called her an "elite," whatever that meant. Perhaps I make her feel like a dummy like her father, Fern reasoned.

Fern was the only girl from Brownies who made the S.P.s. None of the girls she was friendly with would be going with her to Parkchester Junior High School. They would all be going to the neighborhood school together. Only she would be going alone. Still, she was glad she made the S.P.s.

23

Fern looked on as her mother packed her summer clothes in a large suitcase.

"Is that what I have to wear this summer? I don't want those old things!" she complained.

"Who's going to see you?" Ann said. "It's a very basic place."

After the disappointment with Lyle Lake, Ann had found another bungalow colony with a lake.

Later that day, Ann reminded Fern about getting a dog. "If you still want to, you can try again, but it has to be small, black, short haired, and male."

Fern was surprised at how excited she was. Despite what happened with Shadow she still wanted a dog, and suddenly she wanted one more than ever.

At the A.S.P.C.A, she was nervous. They were leaving in a few days, and this was her last chance. The endless aisles of caged dogs were pitiful, and there were no small, black puppies. One puppy jumped up and down trying to get Fern's attention. He had a shaggy white coat and was much bigger than Shadow. Only his eyes and nose were black. Fern called her mother and pleaded. To her surprise, Ann said yes.

Fern named him Teddy because he looked like a Teddy bear. The next few days, she spent every minute petting him, giving him food and water, even watching him sleep. She looked forward to seeing him run through the grass in the country.

At first sight Fisher's Paradise Bungalow Colony lived up to its name. It had wide lawns, lush woods, and a sparkling lake. However, the lake teemed with snapping turtles and the lawns with poison ivy.

As Fern watched Ann set up her portable sewing machine, she asked, "There's nobody my age here - what am I going to do all summer? Maybe you could teach me to sew?"

"What do you think of this?" Ann said, ignoring the question. She held up a large piece of pale yellow cotton with a tiny floral print.

"Oh, no!" Fern exclaimed, remembering the home-made skirt.

"It's not for you, it's for Grandma. I'm making a dress with a zipper down the front so it'll be easier with her arthritis." Ann said with annoyance. "You wanted a dog for so long. Why don't you train him before school starts and you get too busy."

Fern started walking Teddy around the lake every day and often saw George, the handyman. He was nineteen, dark haired, and muscular. He had a lot of work keeping the grounds clean and fixing the old plumbing in the cabins.

Fern screwed up her courage to say hello, but he barely looked at her. She was wearing old corduroy pedal-pushers which were totally out of fashion. Angrily, she remembered her mother's words: "Who's going to see you?" She knelt to pet Teddy, burying her face in his fur and thinking, at least he likes me!

The next day, Fern awoke to find her right eye swollen – it was the size of a baseball. She had read about elephantiasis in "National Geographic," but how could she have gotten it? And what other body parts might start to swell?

Ann rushed Fern to the city where the doctor gave her a shot of cortisone and a crash course in poison ivy.

"You probably got it from your dog," he said. "His fur carries oil from the plant. Wash your hands every time you touch him."

When they got back to Fisher's Paradise, they realized

poison ivy was everywhere. It twined around trees, grew like a bush, and hid amongst innocent plants. When Ann complained, Mr. Fisher threw up his hands and said that it was impossible to get rid of. They had even tried burning it, but the ash made people sick.

"Just stay away from it," he cautioned. "Leaves of three, let them be!"

Fern couldn't hug or kiss Teddy any more, and she had to be careful where she stepped and what her clothing brushed against. Calamine lotion helped, but the ugly red rash on Fern's face and arms persisted. The doctor said it would be gone before her cousin Fernie's wedding. That made Fern feel better. The wedding was to be the highlight of the summer.

The morning of the wedding, the family took turns in the shower and at the mirror. Don had to be watched lest he spoil his new suit, and his shoes were scuffed. There was no shoe polish, so Leo suggested a bit of vaseline. By that time, it was getting late.

"Give Teddy a quick walk before we leave," Ann said.

Fern searched around the cottage but couldn't find him. Nobody had seen him.

" We'll all look - he couldn't have gone far," Ann said. "Let's spread out, everybody in different directions. But come back in ten minutes. We have to leave."

Fern's eyes swept the wide lawns, and she asked everyone she passed. When she returned to the cottage, she said she wouldn't leave until he was found.

"It's getting late, and if we miss our train we'll miss the wedding," Ann scolded. "I'm only giving it another ten minutes."

"I'm going to keep looking," Fern said.

"You better be back in ten minutes, because we're leaving no matter what!"

"You would leave Teddy just for a wedding?" Fern exclaimed. "I don't care if I miss the wedding."

Fern ran out of the cottage towards the woods. She would even go into the forest if she had to. At the edge of the woods, the bungalow colony's trash cans overflowed, and there she found Teddy, munching on a pile of potato peels. The rest of the day was a blur, but Fern would always remember the dog and the wedding - her mother had made the wrong choice!

The summer was almost over when Fisher's Paradise divulged another surprise. On a quiet, lazy afternoon, two screaming figures came running out of the woods. It was Don and his friend Billy, their bodies covered with hornets. They had stepped into a hornet's nest. They ran to their bungalows, shrieking in pain.

Billy's mother refused to let him in because there was a baby in the house. She left him wailing at the door. Ann swatted the hornets off Don's face until Fern had a brainstorm. She suggested putting him into the shower. Under the cold rushing water, the hornets dropped off one by one, their plump, fringed bodies writhing. Don recovered, but Billy had to be brought to a clinic.

When the time came to leave the bungalow colony, the Bookmans waited by the entrance for the car that would take them to the city. The expansive lawn and lush trees were as green as the day they arrived.

"What does he care about poison ivy and snapping turtles?" Ann said bitterly. "Fisher's Paradise is a paradise only in the mind of Mr. Fisher, as long as he gets his rent!"

\ \ \ \ \

As soon as they returned to the city, Ann went with Fern and Don to Grandma's, eager to give her the dress.

"I like this zipper down the front," Grandma said. "Buttons are hard for me now."

"I know, Ma," Ann said, smiling. "You can't find anything like it in the stores. I'm planning to make more from the same pattern."

Ann told Grandma about the incident with Don and the hornets. Fern had heard her tell it before but wanted to hear it again, especially the part that went, "Fern really saved him."

Before they left, Ann told Grandma she had something

important to talk about.

"Ma," she said, "You know we're moving to a new house, and I want you to move too. This place isn't good for you. It's dangerous, and you shouldn't be walking all those stairs. Why would you want to stay here anyway with the shul closed?"

Grandma's face took on a hard look. "Where would I go? The rent is good here."

"You could move to my place when we move out. It's rent-controlled, and the important thing is it's safe."

Grandma shook her head. "I'm all right here. I want to be near Olga."

"If you're waiting for Olga, you'll never move."

Grandma got up from the table and went into the kitchen, signaling the end of the conversation.

"Why did you say that about Olga?" Fern whispered. There had always been something wrong between her mother and Olga, but she didn't know what.

"She's a mixed up person, and her husband is even worse. They take advantage of Grandma's generosity. Even though Olga doesn't work, Grandma baby-sits all the time, and they borrow money which they don't always pay back. Daddy and I have as little to do with them as possible. I don't want to talk about it."

"Olga is going to move," Grandma said when she returned. "We both are. As soon as they build the Soundview Houses."

"Soundview Houses?" Ann said scornfully." It'll take years. They want to build on landfill."

Grandma silently gathered up the dishes and took them to the kitchen.

On the way home, Fern asked if Grandma would ever move.

"I don't know," Ann said. "She shouldn't depend on Olga."

"What is Soundview Houses?"

"It's a housing project they're planning for a marshy part of the Bronx. First they have to do a land-fill project. They may never build it."

Before they moved into their new house, Ann surprised

Fern by asking what color she wanted for her room. Fern said yellow, envisioning a pale, lemon yellow that would fill the room with sunshine.

When move-in day finally came, the Bookmans wandered from room to room like dreamers. There was a long living/dining room which led to a small kitchen. In the rear of the kitchen was a door that opened to a small landing and a flight of stairs down to the garden. Upstairs there were three bedrooms.

Fern's room, at the end of the hall, faced the garden. It should have been perfect, but when Fern opened the door, she gasped. The whole room was a garish canary yellow.

"That's not what I wanted. It's horrible!"

"You had your choice, you said yellow," Ann said. "We're not painting again."

Fern noticed that people passing the house always stopped to admire the huge Peace Roses in the front. They inhaled the scent not realizing they were smelling the nearby honeysuckle. Longingly, Fern looked at the pale, coral tinted yellow of those roses - exactly the shade she wanted. Instead she'd have to live with the ugly yellow of her room until she went away to college.

For a few days, Fern and Don ran up and down the stairs - their stairs! The house was bright and spacious, and as the months went by Fern's disappointment with the color faded. Now, when frictions arose, the family had separate rooms to retreat to. Soon, the apartment on Netherland Avenue became a distant memory.

PART II

24

In Bronx District Office 29, a secretary took a list out of a file cabinet. On her desk was a letter from girl number six in the Special Science class saying she was moving to New Jersey. The secretary circled the first girl on the list and typed a letter:

Dear Fern,

Congratulations! You have been chosen for a new program mandated by the United States Congress to educate future scientists. We are writing to inform you of an opportunity to switch your class assignment to 7SP1, the Special Science Class. In addition to your regular program of studies, you will have two science classes daily and go on frequent field trips, completely paid for by the federal government.

This is a prestigious program. Only the best students have been invited to participate. Please let us know by August 25th if you want to switch your present assignment.

It was already August 20th. The letter had been re-routed from Netherland Avenue. Ann immediately called the district office.

Ann told Fern that other students from Pelham Parkway were in the science class including two girls she already knew, Pamela and Kay. Fern's heart dropped. Of all the girls, it had to be them!

Fern was looking forward to her assigned arts and literature class, and she had learned that in it was a girl from Pelham Parkway she wanted to get to know. She was more upset about the two unfriendly girls than about giving up her original assignment, but she told herself something like that shouldn't influence her.

"We can't tell you what to do," Ann said. "You're the one who'll be there every day, and you're the one who has to decide." But, more than anything Fern wanted her parents to decide. She thought about it the whole next day.

Ann said that when Leo came home, they would talk about it and decide. That night, they all sat at the kitchen table. Fern had no idea what her parents would say.

"I hope it won't cost a lot to send her on the field trips," was the way Ann opened the discussion. It was as if the decision was already made.

"Is that all you can think about?" Fern asked.

Leo reminded Ann that the government was paying for everything. His tone convinced Fern. She would accept the science class.

Fern was proud to be chosen. It was obvious that 7S.P.1 was better than 7S.P.2, and it would make her father happy. She wasn't sure it would make her happy.

When Ann asked if she wanted to go to the bank the next day, Fern was glad of the distraction. They would also go to the nearby Five and Ten Cent Store which she loved.

In the store window, a display of dolls caught her eye. The dolls had porcelain heads, long frilly dresses, and elaborate hair-dos - they looked like they were from the 18th century.

"Come on! What are you wasting time looking at dolls," Ann said. "You're too old for that!"

"I don't want to buy one. I was just looking!"

Fern had totally forgotten the doll she once had, but now she now remembered it. When she was eight, she had asked for a doll only because other girls had them. Ann bought her a large, cheap plastic doll with a chubby body and reddish hair. Fern called it "Connie," a name a cowgirl might have. The novelty of having a doll soon wore off, and it was relegated to the back of the closet.

Now Fern asked, "Where is my doll?"

"You stopped playing with it a long time ago," answered Ann. "I gave it to the Salvation Army so some poor girl could have it."

What about me? Fern thought. I feel like a poor girl. "Where is the Salvation Army?" Maybe we could get it back."

"No. It was a long time ago."

It was her doll, not her mother's, something to pass on to her own daughter, if she ever had one. At the very least, her mother should have told her.

Once in the store, they went to the school supply section and picked out a package of pencils, a small sharpener and a small notebook. Fern asked if she could get a large, red leather pencil case.

"You already have a pencil case. Don't waste money on things you don't need," answered Ann.

Afterwards, they went to the bank which was crowded with long lines. Standing on another line, Fern spotted Kay, also with her mother. Kay's crisp, white summer dress was exactly what Fern wished she had. She decided that if Kay noticed her she would go over and tell her they were in the same class. However, Kay kept her eyes focused on the teller the whole time. When Fern realized Kay had left, she was strangely relieved, but for the next few days, her decision nagged at her.

` ` ` ` `

That weekend, Ann asked Fern if she wanted to go with her to visit her friend in Chappaqua. "I could use the company. Daddy is taking Don to the zoo."

Fern loved getting out of the city. They would pass beautiful homes and lush greenery along Boston Post Road. Unlike the Bronx, in Westchester nature was everywhere.

"I can't wait to see your painting," Fern said as they drove.

" She should have hung it by now, it's been four years," Ann pointed out.

When they got to Jeanette's house, Ann looked for the painting where she had envisioned it, over the fireplace. Instead there was a reproduction of an Impressionist landscape.

"The room looks pretty," Ann said, hoping Jeanette would mention the painting.

"Do you think so? I'm redoing this room; a lot of things I brought up here I'm getting rid of."

"Well those drapes look nice."

"I don't like them, they were good enough for the Bronx, but there's a higher standard here."

"Is that so?" Ann said.

Later, as she served coffee, Jeanette asked about Rockaway. Ann explained what had happened to Rockaway, but instead of commiserating, her friend said, "There's a beautiful country club here, and we're on the waiting list. I could get you in if you ever moved here."

Ann didn't bother to hide her annoyance when she answered, "We just bought a house. Didn't you know?"

Fern began regretting that she had come.

Ann could wait no longer. "By the way, where is the painting I gave you?"

"I don't know what happened to it, things were so disorganized when we moved. Maybe it's in the attic."

"It's been four years, Jeanette. If you're not going to hang it, I'd like it back."

When they finally left, Ann vented her anger. "What a nerve to take my painting and not hang it up! She probably gave it away. Just because she lives in Chappaqua, she thinks she's upper-class. They probably look down on her because her husband runs the stationary store."

For a while they rode in silence, and then Fern said, "You've been friends for a long time, haven't you?"

Ann explained that Jeanette had been one of the members of the Satellite Social Club, and she had known her for more than twenty years. "I was even there when she met her husband,'" she said bitterly.

"Better a certain enemy than an uncertain friend," Ann said as they pulled into their driveway. As they entered the house, she added, "Maybe you'll do a painting someday."

25

Fern carefully brushed her hair and fixed it into a ponytail. She put on her jacket and picked up her bookbag.

"Remember your bus pass," Ann said, handing it and a dollar bill to Fern.

"What's this for?"

"Just in case you need it, but you probably won't."

It was a gray September day. As she walked to the bus stop, Fern noticed the trees along Pelham Parkway were beginning to lose their leaves. The start of the first day - and she was already filled with doubt.

Fern had never before crossed to the other side of the parkway alone. There were four lanes of speeding cars, and she had to walk fast before the light changed. Getting to the other side felt good, but the bus stop was deserted. This wasn't the way things should be.

There was an unwritten rule in the Bronx: "Stay in your own neighborhood." Fern had never been to Parkchester. She had heard something about it, but she couldn't remember what. Suddenly she thought - what if the whole thing is a mistake? But there was no point turning back. Nobody was home anyway.

Her mother's words came to her: "SPS, self - pity stinks!" She continued on to the next bus stop, to White Plains Road where there were always lots of people.

She thought of her friends on their way to the neighborhood junior high, laughing and joking. They weren't thinking of her.

The White Plains Road stop was also deserted, but a line of people on their way to work slowly formed. She asked a woman if the bus went to Parkchester, and when the woman said it did, she felt better.

The minutes went by, but neither Kay nor Pamela appeared. Am I that desperate to want to see them, Fern asked herself. Then she realized that the bus wasn't for them. Royalty must have a coach! They would be driven to school - their fathers had cars. Though they were the only other girls from Pelham Parkway in the Special Science Program, they would still shun her.

When the bus finally came, she showed the driver her pass and asked him to tell her when they got to Parkchester Junior High School. She was the only student on the bus and she took a seat near him.

Stop after stop, she looked for other kids. Finally, a group came running for the bus and boarded through the rear door. The driver said nothing about them sneaking on, and the bus continued. Fern thought that was strange.

The group was noisy and exuberant and clustered around a boy who was a head taller than the rest. His face shone with laughter.

"Tall, dark and handsome," was what her mother had said about her father. "Negro" was what people down South would say, but 'Black' wasn't appropriate either. His skin was the color of maple syrup. What was he like? What did it matter, she thought. It was just a fluke he was on the same bus.

The view out the window changed from a mix of small stores and houses to clusters of tall red brick buildings. "Brick City," would be a better name than Parkchester, Fern thought. It looked like a huge correctional institution. The buildings were all the same. Would the people be the same too?

Now she remembered about Parkchester. It was a planned community that limited the number of Jews and had a "whites only" policy. Could she ever be happy there?

The bus stopped in front of a sprawling, white-columned,

beige brick structure, Parkchester Junior High School. It took up an entire block and looked like an historic building. Fern was glad it didn't look like the other buildings. It could have been anywhere in America.

Students with colorful backpacks streamed up the broad stairs, and Fern realized for the first time that her bookbag was just a cotton bag with a drawstring. In the hallway, a diagram directed her to a second floor classroom. In the room another diagram showed the seating arrangement. She was surprised to find her seat in the front, up against a massive lab table.

A small, gray-haired woman addressed the class. "Good morning students, I am Mrs. Linder, your science and home-room teacher. Like you, I was specially chosen for this program, and I'm very happy to be here. We're all lucky to be here. This new program was created by the federal government to educate future scientists.

"You will have three years of work to do in two, so there's no time to waste. We have our own corner of the school, so it won't take long to change classes. To save time, you will bring your lunch and eat at your desk. Remember, you're not like other students. You have to do things differently."

A rustle went through the room. Fern suspected she wasn't the only one with doubts.

"There will be two science classes every day and a test every two weeks," Mrs. Linder continued. "The year will be divided into four areas: Biology, Chemistry, Geology, and Physics. There will be lots of homework, and if you are absent you have to get notes from another student. All assignments and homework have to be made up within two weeks."

A low laugh, more like a snort, escaped from a boy in the back. Mrs. Linder gave him a sharp look.

"After you copy the list of supplies on the blackboard, I'll introduce you to Mrs. Madison, our very own guidance coun-selor."

After copying the list, Fern looked around. She saw Kay, Pamela, and a few boys she knew. Then a tall, well-dressed woman came to stand next to Mrs. Linder.

"This is Mrs. Madison, who we are very lucky to get."

Fern wondered why they even needed a guidance counselor. In her mother's school they were just for discipline problems.

"You have been specially chosen for this class, and you are
lucky to be here," Mrs. Madison began. "You will go on eight trips
a year. You will visit Brookhaven National Laboratories to see a
nuclear reactor. Also the Benjamin Franklin Museum in Phila-
delphia where you'll sleep in the museum for the night. I'm sure
you'll work very hard to show your appreciation."

Fern was tired of being told how lucky she was.

The day proceeded like a regular day but with shortened
periods, and Fern met all her teachers. English was the last class
of the day, and Miss Shaw flashed a radiant smile as she faced the
class. Fern liked her immediately.

"Today is a hard day for you with a new school and a new
program. I'm going to give you an assignment that will be fun.
At least I hope it will be fun. I want you to write something just
for yourself. Nobody else will see it unless you show it to them.

"Write the story of your life. You don't have to start at
the beginning. You can start with the most important person in
your life or an important event. Write whatever you want because no one will see it but you."

The class stared at her blankly.

"There's a cabinet in my room where I will lock everything
away. At the end of the year, all you have to hand in is any five
pages. That's what I'll grade you on."

"If you can write anything you want, and nobody will see
it, does that mean you can use dirty words?" Every head turned.
With a shock, Fern saw it was Joey Roman.

Miss Shaw smiled, "I meant it when I said your writing will
be private. I want you to express yourself, no holds barred."

That night, as Fern worked on the assignment, she wasn't
sure if she should reveal her true feelings. She lingered a while
before picking up her pen. Then she wrote:

My Father

Early one morning, when I was a little girl, my father woke me up to see a horse-drawn wagon in front of our apartment building. It was parked right between the cars. A big horse with blinders looked like it stepped out of a storybook. The milk wagon was making one of its last rounds. That was five years ago, and now there are no more milk wagons. My father was giving me a history lesson, but I didn't know it.

He helped with my homework, took me to the zoo, and taught me how to throw and catch a ball.

If you were to meet my father, you would never guess he grew up poor. He is tall, good-looking, and well-dressed. He never raises his voice and always has a smile on his face. Although he's not outgoing, people like him. Maybe because he never says anything to upset anyone. He is quiet, but my mother says, "Still waters run deep." For instance, he just told me he used to have a small boat. I was surprised because he never mentioned it before.

My mother said he is a Renaissance man. He's an athlete who swims and plays tennis. In college, he was a boxer and captain of his basketball team. He studied to be a doctor, so he knows a lot about health. He's so interested in what's happening in the world that he gets the morning paper on his way to work and the evening paper on the way home.

My father is the most important person in my life.

That doesn't mean I don't love my mother, but my father is special.

26

Ann was kneeling in front of an old wooden chest that held scraps of fur from Leo's part-time job. There was mink, sheepskin, fox, racoon, and squirrel. Fern had played with them when she was little.

"You don't want these anymore, do you?" Ann asked.

Fern picked up a small, irregular piece and stroked it. She dropped it abruptly when she guessed that the rounded edge was where the leg had been cut off.

"Why do people wear fur?" Fern exclaimed. "We're not in the stone age anymore!"

Ann laughed. "You're right, we don't need it, but it's the warmest thing there is, and it's beautiful."

On a particularly cold day, Fern shivered while waiting for the bus. She reconsidered her attitude about fur, and that evening asked Ann for a fur jacket.

"You're always cold, and now with the bus I guess you need it. I'll ask Daddy. It would have to be mouton. Anything else is too expensive." Ann explained that mouton was a fancy word for sheep and added, "Aunt Adele has a mouton coat."

Fern still wasn't sure about fur, but at least sheep were killed not just for their skin.

All fur coats and jackets were made to order, so Ann took Fern to a furrier to be fitted.

"Which do you want?" asked the short, white-shirted furrier. He pointed to four swatches on a table. Fern chose a dark-tipped pale fur.

"That one is a special process. It costs more," he said.

"We're looking for something basic," said Ann, "just something to keep her warm."

The furrier gave Ann an appraising look. "I'm already giving you a discount. I guess it'll have to be the dark brown."

Fern felt uncomfortable as the man took her measurements. It was like being at the doctor's. A rack of coats in the corner caught her eye. "What are those?" she asked.

"Oh, those are finished, waiting to be picked up," the furrier said dismissively. "There's one other thing, the lining. For a small charge, you can have it monogrammed."

"How much?" Ann asked.

"Fifteen dollars," he said, "It's an elegant touch."

Ann considered for a moment before she answered. "I guess it's O.K. If you left it somewhere, it's like security."

A month later, as Fern waited for the morning bus, it started to snow. Her new coat was warm, but it weighed a ton. She felt like there was a heavy weight on her back.

\ \ \ \ \

After they settled into the house, Sol moved in. One day, Fern asked him about the old country. Leo had almost no memories of it, being only four when he left.

Sol told about the prince and his nearby estate. He fondly recalled collecting walnuts that fell from the prince's trees. Gnarled and brown, he himself reminded Fern of a walnut. Sol's main activity was smoking - he couldn't go for more than two hours without a cigarette. Ann told him to only smoke downstairs in his own apartment, however he would come upstairs during the day when everyone was out. When Ann came home, she detected the odor and became angry. Sheepishly he would promise not to do it again, and for a few weeks the air would be clear.

One day Fern overheard her parents arguing. "Can't you tell him not to smoke in the house?" Ann said. "It's bad enough that it reeks downstairs, he doesn't have to do it up here too!"

"Solly had a hard life. He became a chain smoker during the

war. He said it warded off hunger. Okay Ann, I'll talk to him," Leo said.

There was another point of contention. Sol gave Teddy scraps from the table despite being told not to. One night, as Fern did her homework, she again overheard her parents.

"I can't complain about having to clean his apartment because that was part of the deal, but I don't want him bringing his bad habits upstairs," Ann said.

Fern couldn't hear her father's words, only his conciliatory tone. Having Sol in the house gave her a feeling of family, and she felt sorry for him.

A few months after their move, Aunt Adele and her husband came to see the house. It was the first time anyone in the family had visited, and Ann tidied up furiously.

"Take Teddy for a walk before they come," Ann said.

When Fern got back, Adele and her husband Louis were sitting on the sofa. They were stout and healthy, well matched. Fern had only seen Louis a few times, and the little she heard about him wasn't good. Sol had left the house to avoid him.

"Is that your new jacket?" Adele asked Fern. "Come here, let me have a look."

Fern approached and proudly showed the gold colored lining with the purple monogram.

"Oh, it's beautiful!" her aunt said. "I'm sure you love it."

"It is beautiful," Fern said, "but it weighs a ton."

Adele laughed, but Louis asked Fern to come closer. He stood up and told her to put her arms out. As he fingered the sleeves and the shoulders, he asked, "What size do you wear? Was the jacket made to order?"

"Of course it was," Ann said. "Why are you asking?"

"Because it's too big. See how it hangs from her shoulders? It's supposed to fit snug." Louis laughed. "He gave you a left over jacket. It was made for someone else who never picked it up. Sometimes that happens."

Ann was angry, but Fern believed Louis. The coat was too big, even with all the measurements.

After coffee and cake and a tour of the house, Louis asked to see where Sol lived.

"We better not go down there. Sol isn't home and that's his place," Leo said.

"I guess you don't want to show how you put your brother in the basement," Louis said.

"What do you mean by that?" Leo asked. "It's a finished basement, a regular apartment with windows and its own door."

Louis turned to Adele. "He takes his brother's money and lets him live like a rat in the cellar."

"Louie!" Adele said pleadingly.

"Who are you to criticize?" Leo said. "You may have signed a piece of paper to get him out of Europe, but it didn't cost you a thing. If anyone should have taken Solly in, it was you. Adele is his sister. Ann isn't even related to him, but she does the cooking and cleaning for him. You have some nerve. I want you out of my house!"

Fern had never seen her father so angry. But she was proud of him.

The next day, Fern asked her mother about Louis. "I don't know why he's so mean," Ann answered. "Nobody likes him."

"But why did she marry him? Didn't she know what he was like?"

"People get married for a lot of reasons. Adele was older when she got married. She was afraid she'd be an old maid."

"But why him?"

"He is a good provider. He gave her a four carat diamond ring."

"She married him for a ring?" Fern asked. "That doesn't make sense."

"Adele had a hard life," Ann explained. "She was the oldest girl and had to take care of the other children. Then, when she was a teenager, she brought her younger brother Abe to America. The rest of the family stayed in Europe until there was enough money for the trip.

"On the steamship, Abe spent most of his time on deck

and his eyes became irritated from the soot of the smokestacks. When they landed at Ellis Island, the health inspectors thought he had trachoma, an eye disease. They sent him back to Germany, and Adele had no choice but to go with him. When they landed, Adele was out of money and she went to a park near the dock and began to cry. A kind Jewish man saw her and brought them to his home. He contacted the family and they sent money for them to go back to New York.

"It was very hard for Adele, for all of Daddy's family. We can't understand what it was like because we were born in America."

27

Homeroom was supposed to allow students time to catch their breath, but Mrs. Linder used it to cram in more work. It was just the second week of school, and as soon as Fern entered the room, she saw the blackboard filled with chemical equations.

"Hurry up and copy these. I want them in your notebooks before class today," Mrs. Linder's voice rang out. Fern hadn't even taken off her coat.

The students wondered whether Mrs. Lindner was allowed to start teaching during homeroom. Weren't they supposed to get settled first?

There were seventeen boys and thirteen girls, mostly from Parkchester. Fern knew the boys from P.S. 303. They were smart, but unathletic. It looked like the sun had never touched their faces. The girls were plain looking and serious, the type that would go into science. More than anything, Fern wanted to befriend them.

At 11:30, everyone took out their lunchboxes and paper bags and ate at their desks. A boy sat next to Fern, and next to him sat Kay who was focused on her lunch. Fern wanted to say something to her, but reconsidered. Lunch was over quickly, and students hurriedly gulped their drinks and put away uneaten apples.

Mrs. Linder exhorted the class, "Look at the evidence before you form a conclusion!" She lived and breathed the scientific method.

Fern learned a new way of looking at the world, and for the first time school was challenging. The scientific experiments were fascinating, and the sounds of French felt delicious in her mouth, but by the end of the day, her fingers sore from writing, she was exhausted. She hurried to the bus stop without lingering.

Now that she was studying science, Fern thought her father would be eager to help. There were many things she wanted to talk about, but he was never around. She felt he was avoiding her.

After a frenetic week, it was pleasant to do nothing on the weekend. One Sunday morning, as she sat by the window, Fern was surprised to see Sol rolling a bicycle towards the house.

"I bought the bike for you. It's a very good bike, a folding bike," he said. It was olive green and large, and looked impossible to fold.

"It's army surplus," Sol explained. "It doesn't actually fold, it just comes apart in the middle. Fern was doubtful, but with Sol's urging she was soon riding up and down the block. She wanted her father to see, but he had gone for a long walk. He no longer took his children on Sunday outings.

That night, Fern asked Ann, "Why doesn't Daddy help with my homework anymore?"

"What do you mean?" Ann said. "If you need help, he will. He always does."

"It's not only that. We don't go to the zoo or the botanical gardens anymore."

"You're not a little girl. You can go yourself."

"I don't think Daddy cares about me anymore."

"He doesn't mean anything by it. You're a young woman now, and it's not right for him to spend so much time with you."

"What do you mean, a young woman?" Fern exclaimed. She wasn't a young woman. Even if she was, it wasn't her fault. Why should she be punished for it?

Ann gazed at Fern and shook her head. "We'll talk about it later. Now isn't a good time."

Fern's birthday was celebrated in the usual way, with just her family. Her mother gave her a small box that she was sure must be the scatter pins she wanted, but turned out to be the red pencil case.

Her mother smiled and said, "You see, I remembered! And here's something from Grandma."

Fern was surprised - Grandma only sent cards. She was even more surprised when she opened the box and saw the scatter pins - two tiny ceramic turtles, exactly what she wanted. How did she know? She was sure she had never told her grandmother. She didn't talk to her much at all, and certainly not about frivolous things.

Estelle gave Fern a paperback edition of *The Moon and Sixpence* by Somerset Maugham, the romantic story of the artist Paul Gauguin. The present was unexpected - no other friend remembered her birthday. Estelle thrust the unwrapped book into her hands unceremoniously and said she loved the story and thought Fern would too. Estelle was now living in Manhattan and they only saw each other at art class. Fern felt the book was a bond between them as artists.

As the school term progressed, Fern realized the Parkchester girls had been paired up before they started school. Fern liked Jill, one of the brightest girls in the class, but Jill and red-headed Donna were always together and had been best friends since first grade. Neither took any notice of Fern. From the start of the year, Pamela and Kay seemed to know Jill and Donna. Fern suspected their mothers had organized get-togethers during the summer. A favorite song from Brownies was, "Make new friends, but keep the old/ One is silver, and the other gold." She had neither.

Mrs. Madison, the guidance counselor, addressed the class every few weeks, always talking about her ten year old son, Walter. He was a math whiz, she told the class. His spelling wasn't good, but he had listened to her, had studied, and received 100% on his spelling test. Mrs. Madison ignored a snicker from the back of the room.

After one of her talks, Mrs. Madison asked Fern to step out of the room. Fern assumed it was for an errand, but this was no ordinary errand. Someone was needed to accompany a girl home when she felt sick. Pale, thin, bespectacled Lina lived at the opposite end of Pelham Parkway, and Fern had never noticed her. Fern was flattered to be chosen, and Ann gave her consent.

A week later, in the middle of the day, Fern became a chaperone. She and Lina took the bus in silence, and when they got to the apartment, Lina's mother invited Fern in. The woman walked with a limp, and though she looked nothing like her, she reminded Fern of Aunt Adele. Fern watched how she fussed over her daughter, and she wondered which chronic disease Lina had.

The next day, Mrs. Madison, to Fern's surprise and embarrassment, announced to the class that since Fern would be taking Lina home when she felt sick, someone was needed to take notes for the work they missed.

"Who is willing to do that?" she asked.

Fern squirmed in her seat, but soon Kay's hand shot up.

Mrs. Madison smiled. "Thank you Kay, that is very nice of you. I know you have good handwriting. I'm sure Fern and Lina will be grateful. We can all learn from Kay. She has shown a real spirit of cooperation."

What about my cooperation? Fern thought.

A month later, Lina got sick at the beginning of gym class. Fern hated gym because they always played volleyball which she wasn't good at. She had never been on a team, and she could barely serve the ball. Her class played with girls from a regular class, some of whom were good players. They jeered when other girls missed the ball. Fern was filled with fear just entering the gym. She hoped Lina's sick days would coincide with gym.

For the rest of the school year, Fern accompanied Lina. She was proud to do it and looked forward to stepping into Lina's bright, well-decorated apartment. Kay's notes were neatly written and comprehensive, and Fern suspected she learned more from them than being in class.

28

When Miss Shaw announced a poetry unit, Fern was happy - she had always wanted to learn about poetry. She was impressed that a famous poet, Edgar Allen Poe, once lived in the Bronx. Her favorite poet was Emily Dickinson, whose poem, "I am nobody/ Who are you?/ Maybe you are nobody too," expressed exactly how she felt.

Her classmates were somebodies - the smartest boy, the prettiest girl, best friends Jill and Donna. Only she was a nobody. Some of her classmates didn't even know she was from Pelham Parkway.

At the end of the unit, students had to pick a poem and memorize it. Then they had to recite it for the class. Fern didn't care about winning, she just wanted to be noticed. It took a long time to choose the right poem, but "Sea Fever" expressed her love of Rockaway. For a few weeks, she practiced every day.

On the day of the contest, the class listened intently as students recited their poems. Some of the boys chose little ditties, hardly poems at all. When it was Fern's turn, her heart beat faster.

"I must go down to the sea again," she began and finished the poem perfectly. Her classmates stared at her stonily, and no one said anything that day or the following days. Surely someone had liked it!

She overheard a girl compliment Kay, who had recited robot style. Fern had the uncomfortable feeling her classmates were avoiding her. Two weeks later, a boy sidled up to her and told her that the whole sixth grade in Parkchester was forced to memorize "Sea Fever." Everybody hated it. Why hadn't anyone told her ?

＼ ＼ ＼ ＼ ＼

Fern got used to being alone on the bus but dreaded the morning rides, especially waiting for the bus. Occasionally the noisy group with the smiling boy came on at the back. They were so carefree, and she liked to watch them, but she had too much on her mind to think much about him.

When she got home, there was so much homework, she didn't have time to feel lonely. Exhausted after hours of work, she always felt there was more to do. Once in bed, sleep came instantly, and she always dreamt of a tropical island with palm trees and flowers. At times, she was alone on the beach; at other times, she was a bird soaring over the turquoise sea. In the morning, she awoke refreshed, ready for another day.

Towards the middle of the year, Joey Roman's seat was changed - now he was next to her. She guessed he was placed there for the same reason she was: fewer distractions. She wasn't sure how she felt about it. He was trouble, but he reminded her of Fred.

At lunchtime, Fern asked him what happened with Miss Conley. The knife, he explained, was a little penknife his brother gave him. He was caught showing it off in the cafeteria.

"Did you ever get it back?"

"No, I never saw it again, but boy, was my father mad."

They laughed about how angry Miss Conley got when he asked for it back.

One day, during the bi-weekly science test, which Fern always did well on, Joey nudged her. He wanted to see her test paper. She pushed it towards him so he could see. She would do it just this once. However, Joey began to expect her help every time, and Fern felt trapped. He was no friendlier than before, so she started shielding her paper. She was embarrassed that she had tried to buy friendship.

Occasionally, Fern passed Merle on the street, but there

were no greetings. The last day of school had been the last day of their friendship – the friendship that would never end.

Fern decided to befriend Joanne, a nice-looking girl in her class who lived on the outskirts of Parkchester. She also seemed to be a loner. Joanne was happy to be friends and invited Fern over after school. Soon after, a girl who had never spoken to Fern before, said that no one liked Joanne.

"What do you mean?" Fern asked. "She seems nice to me."

"Well, she isn't," the girl said. "You'll see."

Fern ignored the warning. When Joanne's father picked them up in his car after school and brought them back to a small brick house, she was excited and happy.

"Do you know Patsy?" Joanne asked as they sat in the kitchen drinking soda. "She's getting her ears pinned back. She has cabbage ears." Joanne knew all the girls because she had gone to elementary school with them.

Fern wasn't sure what cabbage ears were, and Patsy's ears were concealed by curly blonde hair. Now she understood why Patsy had lately become the center of attention.

"Did you know she's from Ohio?" Joanne continued.

"How could she be?" Fern asked, "I thought Parkchester was only for people from New York."

"Well, she is. Her father didn't want to leave Ohio because he built a fall-out shelter there, but her mother has a sister in Parkchester."

"Who are you friendly with?" Joanne asked abruptly. Fern was embarrassed to admit she wasn't friends with anyone.

"Who do you want to be friends with?"

Now Fern felt trapped. "Jill seems nice."

"Well what do you think of Betty? I used to be friends with her, but now she's friends with Frances. I don't know why, she's so boring!"

A week later, Fern received an invitation to Joanne's birthday party. Joanne warned her not to tell anyone about the party because there were some girls in the class she hadn't invited. By now Fern understood that Joanne was a mean girl who gossiped about everyone. If they stayed friends, Fern might be next, but she wasn't getting any other invitations, so she decided to go.

It was Fern's first co-ed party, and she was nervous. After the birthday cake, they all went down to the wood-paneled basement that Joanne called the "rec room." She asked for a volunteer to stand by the door to look out for her parents while they played spin the bottle.

Garett, a serious boy from the class volunteered. Fern did not want to play at all, but she felt even worse that out of all the boys, Garrett was the least objectionable.

"Mark, you can take over in the middle so Garrett has a chance," Joanne said. Garett said he didn't mind; he seemed relieved not to have to play.

Fern wanted to go home but couldn't think of an excuse. She hoped she wouldn't be chosen but tried to prepare herself. Should she close her eyes? Could she get away with a kiss on the cheek? When the bottle pointed at her, she tried not to panic. At least it was Mark, Joanne's cousin, not one of the boys in her class. She steeled herself as she saw him lick his thick lips. He leaned over and kissed her on the lips. If only she had a tissue!

It was now her turn to spin the bottle, and she panicked. Her thoughts came quickly. She would never again let anyone kiss her on the lips. Why didn't people rub noses like Eskimos?

"I have to leave, my mother said I had to be home by four," she fibbed, and rushed out of the room.

Fern was relieved to get out on the street. She was exhilarated; she didn't care what Joanne thought! When she got home, she wondered if anticipating a party was always more fun than the actual event.

A few days later, Fern saw Joanne looking at her in class, and she turned away. When school was over, she wouldn't have to see her or Parkchester for two whole months.

29

Sol sat hunched over an old carved chess set. Fern had seen him play chess alone before.

"Could you teach me?" she asked.

Sol patiently explained the different pieces and their moves. Fern knew Russians had a fondness for chess but never thought her uncle was smart enough. He had worked as a fur cutter, the lowliest job in the fur business.

When she learned the moves, they started playing, but she never won. Her uncle's horses kept jumping around, and Fern couldn't guess where they would go. Horses were tricky. She knew that.

The more Fern thought about her father's argument with Louis, the angrier she became. Her parents were the only real family Sol had. No one came to visit him. No one cared. She worried that the incident with Louis might end their visits to Adele, but when Passover came they set out as usual.

On entering her aunt's apartment, Fern looked around - Louis wasn't there. As usual, they all settled into the comfortable living room.

Fern listened to Adele talk about her son Laurence who had just returned from basic training in the army. When he strode into the room, tall and fit, Adele got up and took his arm.

"Come over here, so we can look at your new uniform!" she said proudly.

Fern admired Laurence in his crisp khaki uniform- she was

proud to have a cousin who was a soldier. Laurence explained to Don what the stripes stood for and then took out a switch-blade knife which he demonstrated. Fern, on the piano bench, felt left out, but soon Laurence approached her.

"I know how to give an Indian burn. Would you like to see?"

Fern was flattered just to be noticed. She nodded her assent, even though she wasn't sure what an Indian burn was.

Laurence circled her arm with his hands and turned them in opposite directions. He looked her squarely in the face and smiled. Her arm burned, and she expected him to stop, but he didn't. She wanted to act grown up, but when she could take no more, she told him it hurt.

"It's supposed to hurt," he said, his smile broadening. "Don't you know what an Indian burn is?"

The adults now looked up, and Laurence abruptly stopped. "We're just playing around," he said.

Fern's arm was bright red and continued to burn.

Flashing a grin, Laurence headed for the door. He explained he wanted to see his friends before his leave was up.

Fern couldn't wait to get home and run cool water over her arm.

` ` ` ` `

The new house was just a block from Marilyn, and Fern passed her house every day on her way to school. Now that they went to different schools, they never saw each other, and Fern missed her. One day, Fern gathered her courage to visit. As she rang the bell, she wondered if it was a mistake, but as soon as she entered the house, she saw that everything was the same – the mother's frosty greeting, the immaculate room, the girls reading magazines, and Marilyn's warm welcome.

" Oh it's Fern," Marilyn exclaimed delightedly. "How's your new school?"

"Good," Fern said, "except it's in Parkchester."

"How do you get there?" Millie asked. When Fern explained, she asked: "If you take the bus at White Plains Road, doesn't it go along Fordham Road where the Fordham Baldies are?"

Fern had heard of the gang; it was one of many in the Bronx.

"Do you know what they do to girls?" Millie continued, "They come up from behind and cut off their ponytails! They always carry scissors."

Marilyn said that was just to scare girls, it wasn't true, but Fern suspected she only said it to be nice.

"I'm taking art lessons at the 92nd Street 'Y,'" Fern said, changing the topic.

"Who takes you there?" Marilyn asked.

"Nobody, I go by myself. I take the train, it's only half an hour."

"You mean your mother lets you go alone?" Millie asked. Marilyn, whose father had a car, said she had never even been on a train, and to Fern's relief, everyone started talking about trains.

As the conversation waned, the girls got back to their magazines. Fern reached for "True Romance" and chose the story, "My Romance With a Soldier." As she began, she had the feeling she already read it, but when she checked the date, she saw it was the latest issue. They're all the same, she realized. Everything was the same at Marilyn's, yet different. The pink and white room, with its fake French Provincial furniture, was no longer charming.

30

Fern rarely saw her parents disagree, but when Ann announced she was getting a car, Leo objected.

"You can get anywhere you want by public transportation," he said.

"Hilda Schuman was mugged on her way to the subway, and I don't feel safe walking to work through the neighborhood," Ann explained. "And I'm tired of relying on someone to take me to the teachers' luncheons. Now that we have a garage and I'm working, there's no reason not to get one. It'll save time getting to work too."

For several months, Ann took driving lessons. Then, one day, Fern came home from school and saw an old red and white Chevrolet in front of the house.

"It looks like a piece of junk," Leo said when he came home from work.

"It doesn't look like much, but it works fine," Ann responded. "It has a lot of new parts, and I don't want a car that looks good. A teacher's car was stolen last year, but no one will steal this."

"What if it breaks down?"

Ann was annoyed. "I need this car. If it breaks down, I'll have it fixed. Besides I'm not using it for anything but work."

Once Ann started driving, she liked her job even more. At dinnertime she talked about the diamonds and rubies Mary Ann wore and the new guidance counselor, Mr. Goody, who she had become friendly with. Fern thought it was a joke, but Ann assured her that was his real name.

"The amazing thing is he lives up to his name. He is very good. Since he came to the school there are a lot less fights. He knows how to handle the tough kids because he was a marine. He's tough, but he's fair. Everyone likes him."

More and more, Ann spoke about Ralph, the monitor who helped in the office one period a day. One evening, she explained why Ralph was so important to her.

" I was very busy today, and I gave Ralph a message to deliver, but I said Mr. Korchak and I should have said Mr. Korman. It was a payroll form. Luckily, Ralph looked at the name on the envelope and gave it to the right teacher. It was confidential, and I could have gotten into trouble. He's such a help."

"He must come from a good family," Leo commented.

"He lives alone with his grandmother, and he helps her too. Every day he wears a perfectly ironed white shirt. One day I asked how many shirts he had, and do you know what he said?

"He told me he has only one shirt. He washes it every night and irons it in the morning!"

"Where are his parents?" Fern asked. She had never even used an iron.

"I don't know. It's hard to imagine how hard life is for the kids at my school."

Fern was glad her mother was happy but she wished it was she who was making her happy, not the job.

` ` ` ` `

On the last day of class, there were excited whispers as Miss Shaw handed back the year-long writing assignment.

"I promised I'd return them. Look them over and see if your writing has changed."

Miss Shaw was true to her word about handing in only five pages. She said they could keep the rest. Then she gave them their summer assignment.

"I want you to think about this borough where you live. That's why I put those quotes on the board. Which describes the way you feel? You can write anything you want as long as it's about the Bronx."

The quotes were:

"THE INVISIBLE HAND OF THE ALMIGHTY FATHER SURELY GUIDED ME TO THIS BEAUTIFUL COUNTRY, A LAND COVERED WITH VIRGIN FORESTS AND UNLIMITED OPPORTUNITIES"
Jonas Bronck, 1640

"THE BRONX, NO THONX."
Ogden Nash, 1931

"Can it be about Parkchester?" Donna asked.

"Of course," Miss Shaw said. "Since most of you live in Parkchester, it would make a wonderful subject!"

When Fern got her report card, she was proud; she got all 'A's and 'B's. She had mastered complex equations, chemical formulas, French conjugations, and the scientific method. It had been hard.

That night, at dinner Leo complimented Fern. "You did well. Do you think you want to go into science?"

Fern hated biology because thinking about the body was worrisome. Chemistry, her father's major, was boring. She did like geology, but she wasn't sure what a geologist did. She had never met one and probably never would.

"I'm not sure I want to be a scientist" was her answer.

"Well, something happened to me today," Ann said, "and you'll never believe it."

Fern expected to hear more about Ralph or Mr. Goody, but she heard something completely different.

"You know the last day of school is the busiest. I have to get all the files in order and lock them up. I'm the last one to leave, so I have to lock the school up too."

"I didn't know your job was so important," Fern said.

Ann continued: "I was walking to my car in the parking lot, at the far end. It was the only car left- everyone had gone.

I couldn't believe it! All the wheels were off. They were on the ground. A group of teenaged boys was sitting nearby and grinning. I couldn't help myself: I burst into tears!"

Fern saw her father's expression. Was he angry at what happened or at Ann for getting the car in the first place?

Now Ann smiled. "Believe it or not, seeing me cry must have softened their hearts. They put the tires back on!"

Her father still looked angry, but Fern had never been so proud of her mother.

\ \ \ \ \

It was summertime and the plants around the house were blooming. Fern sat by the window and watched the birds pick at cherries on the neighbor's tree. She hadn't even known fruit trees grew in the Bronx. Although it had been a year, Fern still marveled at being in the house.

Ann was singing as she worked in the kitchen. Though the room wasn't large, the window facing the garden flooded it with light.

The doorbell rang, but when Fern went to the door, all she saw was a bunch of huge green leaves on the landing. Ann sometimes lent her hose to two old Italian men who had a truck garden at the end of the block, and the Swiss chard was their way of saying thank you.

Fern decided to go out to the garden, her garden, and look around. It was a small patch of grass which, at the far end, had a low wooden fence. On the other side of the fence, stood an old woman smiling at her.

"When I moved here thirty five years ago, this was all wild," the woman said, making a wide gesture. "There were blackberry bushes and foxes running around." Fern pictured a lush, wild place. "It's all built up now," the woman finished sadly.

Fern thought about Netherland Avenue. By comparison, she was in the country now.

31

A summer without swimming was too much for Ann, so when Nadia told her about an inexpensive hotel in the Catskills, she was interested. The brochure for Brustein's Farm Hotel had a picture of a small, beautiful lake in front of a large white clapboard building. The place had been converted from a farm to a hotel when it became more profitable to take guests from the city than raise cows.

Fern and Don were looking forward to seeing the animals, and Fern anticipated playing with Nadia's daughter, who was two years older. Everyone but Leo, who didn't like hotels, was excited to go.

As soon as they arrived, they were all impressed with the expansive lawns dotted with tall trees, and the mountainous setting.

Ann couldn't wait for a swim, and she and Nadia immediately got into their bathing suits. With their families looking on, they took tiny steps into the cold water of the lake.

"Watch out for the waves!" yelled Nadia's husband Bob, a corpulent, middle-aged man who was always joking.

When the water reached their ankles, they paused. When it was up to their calves, they prepared to plunge in. Another step, then another..... and it got shallow. Brustein's "lake" was a water hole originally dug for the animals.

"At least there's no danger of drowning," Bob said.

Nadia's daughter had changed her mind and wasn't coming, and Fern had a bad feeling about the place.

The other guests didn't mind the lack of activities. They came for the fresh air and the food. The Catskills was all about the food. Between meals, sitting around the lake was all the activity they needed. When Ann told the owner how disappointed she was, he said: "You're the first person who ever complained about the lake."

Meals were served at large round tables, and conversation was lively. Many guests had been coming for years and felt like family.

Unlike Don, Fern, at twelve years old, had just made it to the adult tables. Whereas he had only two choices for every meal, Fern had endless choices. Did she want omelettes, pancakes or cereal? Orange juice, grapefruit, pineapple, or prune? Chicken, meat, fish, or the vegetarian entree? It was like a quiz, especially with her father looking on.

Dinner began with a half grapefruit with a maraschino cherry on top. It was like getting desert first.

"Don't eat the cherry," Leo cautioned, "it has red dye."

Every night, he told the waiter: "I want a plain baked potato and a lean piece of meat." Sometimes he sent the food back. When other men ordered two entrees, he looked on with disgust.

As they waited to be served, someone asked if Brustein's was still a working farm.

"It used to be a big dairy farm, but now they only have about ten or twelve cows," an elderly man volunteered. "There's a farmhand living in the barn who looks after them."

"Could I go and see?" Fern asked.

"I'd be careful around the farmhand, he was away at college for a long time, only been back a few months," the man said.

"It's too late to go to the barn," her father said.

The next day at breakfast, Nadia asked about the farmhand.

"I don't understand. Someone said he went away to college, but he doesn't look like the college type to me."

Laughter burst from around the table.

"Up here in the Catskills, when you say someone went away to college, it means they went to prison," someone explained.

Fern wondered why a criminal would be allowed to take care of animals. Leo said the man was probably raised on a farm and knew all about animals. "When people get out of prison, they can't get a job. He might be working just for room and board."

"I really want to see the animals, can't we please go to the barn?" Fern pleaded.

"The man's an ex-con, we don't know what he did. You better stay away," Leo warned her.

During the day, Ann and Nadia had lots to talk about, and Bob smoked his cigar and dozed in an Adirondack chair, but Leo's favorite activity was long, solitary walks. He loved the clean mountain air.

On Wednesday night, after dinner, the dining room was cleared and set up for the "Silly Hat Contest." Women teamed up to create a wearable hat in twenty minutes, using cardboard, paint, feathers, and other random materials. The guests, many of whom worked in the garment industry, loved to watch the women frantically race against time. Fern had never seen her mother so animated.

The room was silent when it came time to judge. The women modeled the hats, and the audience marked their ballots.

A gray hat with blue feathers looked professional; it was voted most beautiful. Then, the ugliest, silliest, and most colorful were awarded prizes. Fern expected her mother to be disappointed at not winning anything, but she glowed with excitement.

The hats were to be auctioned off, the proceeds going to the waiters who were college students. When her mother's hat came up, Leo bid three dollars and won.

When the ugliest hat came on the block, Bob yelled, " I'll take it for three dollars, I mean you'll have to pay me to take it."

"Hey, my wife made that! I'll give you five to take it!" a man shouted, and the room filled with laughter.

Every day, Fern and Don cast about for things to do. There was nobody Fern's age, and she asked Ann if she could walk with Leo.

"I guess so," Ann said.

"But I don't want to walk along the road," Don piped in.

Fern complained, "It's not fair. I can't go anywhere without him! Just because he doesn't want to, I can't?"

In the end, it didn't matter because Leo had slipped away noiselessly. Like at home, he was in his own world.

"I know I'm not supposed to go into the barn, but can I at least go to the corral and look at the horses?" Fern pleaded.

Ann agreed, and Fern started out with Don tagging along.

At the corral, a lone horse nibbled idly on tufts of grass. The huge barn doors were open, and sitting on a bale of hay was the farmhand. Quietly he eyed them.

He was small and fortyish, his face browned by the sun. He wore a little cap and was neatly dressed. Whenever Fern looked at him, he got busy with his whittling.

Finally, he asked if they were staying at the hotel. Where else would they be staying? Fern thought. There was nothing but woods all around.

As long as she didn't go into the barn, there was nothing wrong with talking to him. She asked about the cows and other animals, and he answered her as if she was an adult.

"Are there any bears around?" she ventured to ask.

"Yep," he said with a wry grin, "sure there are bears, this is the mountains. Are you afraid of bears?"

Fern looked towards the thick woods, and as if to defy him, asked if there were any trails nearby.

"There's a little path along a stream, across the road from the hotel," he said.

As Fern walked towards the hotel, she wondered if any of the guests ever went to the barn. It was only a short walk. They certainly wouldn't go on a trail through the forest.

When she got to the path, she hesitated at first, but there

was nothing wrong with taking a short walk. The little trail ran along a clear stream edged with wild irises. It looked very inviting.

"Let's go," she said to Don.

The trail was narrow so they went single file, Fern in front. She had never been in a forest. It was a world of green with yellow-green stalks and moss covered rocks by the stream. On the other side, tall, dark pines crowded together.

After a while, they stopped. All was quiet except for the occasional bird call. Fern had gone farther than she intended. She stood still and looked around, thinking: what would it be like to live in the forest?

"Let's stay here a moment," she said.

Then there was a crash. Something was moving rapidly, crashing through the underbrush.

"A bear!" Fern cried. "Run, run as fast as you can!"

Don ran, and Fern followed.

It got louder. Something, or someone, was chasing them. As Fern ran, the bright leaves became a blur. Then she remembered the farmhand's knife.

Don was running fast and cried out, "I'm tired, I can't run anymore!"

"You have to! Push yourself," Fern shrieked. "Do you want to get killed?"

He was slowing her down, but if the bear or whatever it was got her, Don could escape. She had brought him, and now she would protect him. Then she realized if he fell and hurt himself, all would be lost. Maybe it was just a deer.

"All right," she said, "you can stop running, but walk fast!" Surely they were close to the road by now.

The sound was still there, but fainter. Then there was a faint whoosh, perhaps the sound of a car.

"We're almost there. I think we're O.K.!"

Finally they saw the road. Fern cautioned Don that, if asked, he was to say they just took a walk. He was never to say they went into the forest.

Fern stayed close to the hotel for the rest of the vacation.

On their last night at Brustein's, there was a dance. Fern lay awake in bed waiting for her parents to return but soon fell asleep. She was awakened by her mother's muffled voice.

Ann was laughing. "Did you ever see so many women dancing with women? What's wrong with these men? Don't any of them dance?" Fern heard her father's deep, soft voice, followed by her mother's laugh again. "I guess I'm lucky to always have you to dance with."

Fern was glad her parents had a good time. Brustein's hadn't been so bad, but she was happy to go home. She fell back to sleep wondering if someday she would have someone to dance with.

In the morning, Ann confronted her.

"I know you went into the woods. I'm not saying how I know, that isn't important. You could have gotten lost, and no one would have known. How would we find you? Did you think of that? And what about Don?"

Fern was close to tears. She knew she shouldn't have taken her brother, but everything had turned out all right.

Ann was throwing things in a suitcase as she said, "This place looks nice, but looks can be deceiving. How can they advertise a lake that's only three feet deep?"

"I hate this place," Fern agreed. "I wish we had never come. It would have been better to stay home."

"You're complaining? We came here because of you. I wanted to get you out of the city. What an ingrate!"

But I was agreeing with her. Why is she turning on me? Fern wondered. Then she exploded with anger.

"You told me there would be lots to do! Nadia's daughter was supposed to come. There was no swimming, no games. I couldn't even go to the barn. What was I supposed to do? We're in the country. You're supposed to be able to go for walks! Daddy always does."

As they drove away, Fern took a last look at the hotel. The farmhand was standing in front, and she didn't want him to see her. She quickly turned her head.

"From now on we'll stay home, so you won't be disappointed," Ann said.

"You don't even care about me," Fern muttered.

When she thought about it later, she was glad she took that walk. She would never forget it.

32

A week before school started, Fern asked Ann for help with her summer writing assignment.

"It's about Parkchester. Everyone thinks it's so great, but I don't."

Ann related the history of Parkchester and added: "You know Grandma applied for an apartment when it was first built, but they turned her down."

After that, Fern had no trouble with her composition.

Parkchester

There are some beautiful parts of the Bronx like The Botanical Gardens, City Island, and The Grand Concourse. Pelham Parkway is a good place to live and so is Parkchester. At least the people who live there think so.

Much of the Bronx was old and crime-ridden when Parkchester was built in the 1940s. It was advertised as affordable housing for working-class people. Those in bad neighborhoods in the Bronx were promised new apartments in Parkchester which has more than 12,000 apartments.

My grandmother lives in the South Bronx in an old, run-down, fourth floor walk-up apartment. When she came to this country, she had nothing. She and her family worked hard to build New York City. She should have been first on the list to get an apartment. However, my grandmother wasn't deemed eligible.

A social worker came to visit. My grandmother's apartment is always spotless. She set out a cup of coffee and a piece of home-made cake.

Instead of helping people in the Bronx, they gave apartments to families as far away as Ohio. As long as you fit the profile. All the people had to be alike, the same as the buildings.

Parkchester was advertised as a real American commmunity, but it's built on prejudice. I'm glad I don't live in Parkchester.

A few weeks after school started, Donna invited Fern over after school. Fern's first thought was that she would finally see the inside of a Parkchester apartment. She chided herself for being disappointed it wasn't Jill, but maybe the invitation would blossom into friendship.

Donna started fretting about her sister as soon as they neared the entrance to the building.

"She's in high school, and she usually goes out with friends after school. I hope she's not home."

Fern barely listened as they entered the apartment. Though nicer than her old one, it looked plain.

In the living room, a teen-aged boy and girl were on the couch.

"Who are you?" Donna asked. The girl answered they were friends of Donna's sister.

"Don't go into the bedroom," the girl said. "Your sister told me to tell you."

Fern could see Donna was upset. They went to the kitchen for a drink. When they came back to the living room, the boy and girl were making out.

"I'm going into the bedroom," Donna declared loudly.

"Are you sure?" Fern asked.

Donna knocked before opening the door. Peering in the

room, she shouted, "You better put your clothes back on!"

Fern peeked into the room. A teenaged boy and girl lay on the bed, fully clothed.

The sister sprang up yelling, "Liar, you know we have our clothes on!"

"But I know what you're doing!" Donna said triumphantly.

"We didn't do anything," her sister answered indignantly.

After that day, Donna avoided Fern, but Fern didn't care any more. She was disgusted with Parkchester and everything about it.

\ \ \ \ \

A highlight of the Special Science Class was the trip to Long Island to see the nuclear reactor at Brookhaven National Laboratory. The class had recently completed a unit on atomic energy and was eager to see a real reactor.

Fern was worried about radioactivity, but her immediate concern was who she would sit with on the bus. As soon as she got on, she looked around. Was Jill motioning to her? Then she remembered Donna was absent.

Fern sat with Jill on the trip there and back, and they talked the whole way. Jill loved mathematics and was especially interested in prime numbers. Fern didn't even know what a prime number was, and Jill's explanation fascinated her. It made Fern realize the science program was geared for students like Jill.

The tour guide reassured the class that they were safe from radiation; they were behind a protective shield. She demonstrated the use of a Geiger counter, then explained the many uses of radiation: in medicine, scientific research, and even food preservation.

Fern was glad when she finally got out on the street. She enjoyed the tour, but her conversation with Jill was what she remembered.

\ \ \ \ \

A few days later, a birthday invitation from Lina came as a surprise. They never talked in school or even on their trips. Fern thought Lina didn't like her. Now she wasn't sure.

The only activity at the party was sitting around the dining room table eating cake and watching Lina open presents. There were no boys, and most of the girls were from her class. It was like a party for a little girl with everything pink.

From the moment she arrived, Fern wondered who she would talk to and if her small gift was appropriate All she could afford was a manicure set. She was relieved when Lina thanked her the same as she did everyone else.

Fern watched the other girls. They had probably given parties she hadn't been invited to. She felt more of an outsider than ever and was sure Lina invited her only out of politeness.

After the party, Fern's job as chaperone soured. She was the only one who took the bus to school - that was why they had picked her. Mrs. Linder was always saying there was so much to learn and so little time, but what about her time? What if something happened on the way back? What if the Fordham Baldies were there?

A week later, Fern was called to Mrs. Madison's office. It was the first time she had been summoned. Was it about Lina? She hated being a chaperone but couldn't bear the ignominy of being dismissed.

Mrs. Madison sat upright behind her big wooden desk and peered over her glasses. "Fran," she said, " I want to talk to you about something."

"Fern, my name is Fern."

"What?" Mrs. Madison shuffled the papers on her oversized desk.

"Oh, yes, Fern, of course. I'm sorry, I've been so busy with this paperwork." Again, she stared at Fern. "Do you wear lipstick?"

Had she heard right? Fern wanted to assure the guidance counselor.

"I never wear lipstick, I don't even have lipstick!"

In the moment of silence that followed, Fern remembered how, long ago, her mother had accused her of wearing rouge.

"Well, maybe you should," the guidance counselor said,

"you're so pale." Then she added more softly, "Is it because you don't have the money? I'd be glad to buy it for you."

Fern averted her eyes. When she looked up, she saw the ornate carving on the desk and realized Mrs. Madison had brought her own desk from home.

"I don't like lipstick," she said.

The guidance counselor pursed her lips as she said, "You can go back to class now."

When Fern left, she went to the Girls' Room and stood in front of the long mirror that ran above the sinks. Frosted windows threw a cool light over the room. She was pale, but who was Mrs. Madison to lecture on beauty? Red lipstick like her mother wore wouldn't look good on her anyhow.

She unfastened her pony-tail to neaten it, and her thick, dark hair spread out around her face. There was another girl at the mirror who had silky, coal-black hair. In that instant, Fern realized that her own hair, which she had always proudly thought black, was plain brown. Just like everyone elses.

` ` ` ` `

A few weeks later, Fern had just gotten to school and hung her jacket in the wardrobe when she saw Lina abruptly stand up, her face ashen. Fern was annoyed; now she'd have to go back.

They didn't speak for the whole trip, and when they got to Lina's apartment, Fern didn't go in. On the way back, she thought about Donna and Jill. The bus stopped and jolted her from her thoughts.

"Wait, I'm getting off!" she yelled.

In her rush, Fern stumbled and fell onto the pavement. She scraped her leg badly and it was bleeding. When she hobbled into the office, the school secretary exclaimed, "What happened to you?"

The school nurse cleaned and bandaged the wound and sent Fern back to the office to wait for her mother. Though it stung, Fern was more shocked than hurt.

"What happened?" Ann asked, as she hurried in twenty

minutes later. The secretary motioned her to take a seat.

"I don't understand how your daughter got hurt. I have to fill out an accident report. What was she doing on the bus at ten in the morning?"

Ann briefly explained the situation.

"So, roughly once a month your daughter takes this girl home in the middle of the day? It sounds like the girl was getting her period."

Fern looked up sharply. So that was it! She felt tricked. Lina didn't have cancer or diabetes.

The secretary continued harshly. "Did you give permission for your daughter to leave school and then come back alone? Weren't you worried about her traveling alone on the bus?"

Ann replied weakly that the school thought it was all right, and Fern wanted to help.

"Would you like to go home?" Ann asked Fern. "I can take you, but then I have to go back to work."

"I feel better, I want to go back to class," Fern said.

That evening Annsaid she wouldn't have to take care of Lina anymore.

"It's not your responsibility. I called the school. Now let them find someone else."

33

One day, as the girls filed into the gymnasium after changing into their gym clothes, Donna went to the door to speak to someone instead of taking her place on the volley-ball court.

"What's going on?" the teacher shouted as she strode to the door. Soon after, Donna left the gym crying.

Fern overheard girls talking about a plane crash. What was it all about? Was she the only one who didn't know?

"Didn't you hear?" a girl said to her. "There was a plane crash and Ritchie Valens died. You know, the one who sings, 'Oh Donna.' Donna was in love with him."

Fern hadn't known. She didn't even know the name of the singer, though she liked the song. She had heard it on the radio. Ann said it was too expensive to get a record player because you'd have to keep getting records. Besides, you could hear the same thing on the radio.

Not having a record player had never bothered Fern before. Now it hit her with full force. She didn't have what her classmates had, she didn't know what they knew. She had never felt so left out.

Fern's feelings were about to change, but she had no inkling of it a day later when Mr. Burke made an announcement in in Social Studies.

"Your class has been chosen to do a presentation on Negro History Week. We'll have to pause our unit on The Treaty of Versailles, and start preparing,"

" Do we have to? What is Negro History Week anyway?" a boy called out.

"Every class must do a holiday for Friday assembly, and that's our assignment. You're smart kids, you'll figure it out. And Miss Shaw will help."

Everything changed in Mr. Burke's class and for Fern it was like a reprieve. By the time the project was over, her feelings about the class and her place in it had also changed.

Mr. Burke wanted the class to be responsible for every part of the production. "I've broken it into three scenes, the slave auction and emancipation, the birth of the Blues, and Jazz. I'll appoint someone in charge of each scene, and you can volunteer for whichever parts you want."

Nearly every boy wanted to portray Abraham Lincoln, including Joey, but he settled for the mute role of a slave on the block.

"Sometimes I Feel Like a Motherless Child," was the saddest song Fern ever heard. Miss Shaw played it over and over so the class could learn it. There were other songs too, all from the album "Negro Spirituals from the Old South." Fern loved every one of them.

Instead of organized lessons, the class met in small groups. Hesitation gave way to excitement. Ideas flew and were shot down rapidly with no ill feelings. The class, always so serious, became animated. In this new experience, new attitudes and approaches were born. Fern was filled with ideas - she was part of the group. She finally felt she belonged.

The performance began with a dark stage and a spotlight on Joey. Head bowed, he stood on a raised platform while the other "slaves" (including Fern) circled round singing the motherless child song. It was a dramatic scene, but Fern wasn't sure it was right. Were they exploiting the slaves' suffering for entertainment?

In the second act, Donna sang "The Birth of the Blues," and in the last act, five girls, including Fern, did a dance that Jill choreographed. Fern felt comfortable working with her classmates. She had never interacted with them for such a long, concentrated time, and she was impressed with their creative abilities.

The class worried about their reception. Fern worried too. The other students in the school were unknown to her. Instead of empathy, the show might provoke laughter or scorn. Judging by the applause though, it was a success. At the very least, Fern thought, it got the students thinking about a terrible time in America's history.

The following Monday, the class expected accolades from Mr. Burke, but all they got was: "Now we can finally get back to The Treaty of Versailles."

The feeling of camaraderie faded quickly, and Fern felt disheartened.

34

M ore than the class itself, Fern looked forward to seeing Estelle at the Sunday morning art classes. The concerts, museums, and art events that Estelle told her about made it sound like Manhattan was exciting, unlike the Bronx. I'm stuck here now, Fern thought, but someday I'll live in Manhattan.

Estelle was one of the best in the class art came easy for her. Fern was improving, but she was getting tired of always drawing boxes, vases, and flowers.

"When are we going to have live models?" was a question everyone was asking.

"What is the difference between naked and nude?" Felicia began, by way of an answer. "Adam and Eve were nude. They didn't have clothing, so they didn't have shame. People started covering their bodies because they felt ashamed of being naked. I want you to understand that because from now on we will have live models."

The human body was beautiful: perfectly balanced and symmetrical, as shown in Leonardo DaVinci's diagram in her art book. Why then did the model in front of the class have a body that sagged and bulged? Fern wondered what made a mature women desperate enough to display her body to a class of thirteen year-olds. By the end of the term, live models were no longer special for anyone.

Felicia promised a surprise for the last class, and the girls assumed it was a party, but when the day came, there were no balloons or decorations.

"Maybe there'll be treats," one girl suggested.

"The surprise is that you're going to have a male model," Felicia announced.

The girls gasped.

"You mean clothed, right?" one girl said.

"No," Felicia answered, "nude."

"But not totally nude," the girl insisted.

"Yes, totally nude! You've been doing nudes for a while, and I think you're old enough."

The girls yelled out objections, but Felicia said, "It's not a choice."

"I'm leaving!" one girl said, heading towards the door.

"Me too," said another, following her.

Fern expected Estelle to stay, but she went too. They all took the elevator to the lobby where they stood in a group, bewildered. One girl called her mother and asked to be picked up, but in the end, the rest trooped back to the room.

The young man on the model stand was not totally nude, but he wasn't clothed either. Fern admired his muscular body; it was symmetrical like the art book illustration. She didn't feel sorry for him.

` ` ` ` `

Felicia was having her first New York art exhibit at Conners Hall of Events. It was an hour's train ride to Greenwich Village, but Ann said Fern was old enough to go herself. She would meet Estelle there. This was her first art opening and she wasn't sure what to wear. After much thought, she settled on a white blouse and plaid skirt, the newest items in her hand-me-down wardrobe.

When Fern checked the invitation and then looked up at the building, she saw it wasn't a regular art gallery as she expected, but a church. A sign directed her to the church basement where another sign read:

CONNERS HALL of EVENTS

A place where artists, dancers, musicians, writers,
puppeteers, and all creative people
who care about their fellow-man, can express
themselves without censorship.
Felicia Forman, Director

The artwork was new to Fern - comic book style naked men and women in all sorts of positions. Was that allowed in a church, and was it considered art? The "art" was drawn on brown wrapping paper tacked to the wall. It fluttered slightly as people passed by.

The large exhibit space was filled with people standing in clusters. They sipped wine from paper cups and talked loudly. No one was looking at the art. Mostly it was men wearing colorful sweaters and scarves, dungarees and tee-shirts. A few wore suits and ties.

Fern immediately spotted Estelle who stood out in a sophisticated dark pink sheath that her mother, an expert seamstress, had made. Heads turned for Estelle, and Fern was painfully aware of her own outfit.

"Isn't it terrible?" Estelle whispered to Fern. "I don't know what to say to Felicia." She had started baby-sitting for Felicia, and they had a close relationship. Fern thought she was the only one who didn't 'get it' and was relieved that her friend disliked the exhibit too.

A young, good-looking man approached and put his arm around Estelle. "This is Damian," she said with a smile.

The man said something to Fern, but his accent (Irish or Scottish) made it hard to understand. When he turned to Estelle, Fern saw her opportunity and headed for the door. Estelle had never mentioned Damian.

As Fern reached the street, she realized she hadn't even greeted Felicia, so she turned back. She stood at the entrance to the hall trying to spot her, but Felicia wasn't mixing with the crowd; she was seated in a corner with her new-born baby. Fern quickly headed towards her. She was relieved that the conversation centered around the baby, and she left as soon as she could.

At last on the street, Fern walked quickly, but she hadn't gone far before Estelle caught up to her.

"I'm glad I got you," she said, "I'll walk you to the subway."

"What about the exhibit? Fern asked.

"I'm going back: there's a party at Felicia's later and I'm going with Damian. I told my mother I was going home with you to sleep over. I don't think she'll call, but I gave her your number. If she does call, just say I'm there but can't come to the phone. Then call me."

"Sure," Fern said. "But who is Damian?"

"He's an artist from Scotland, a friend of Felicia's. I think he's going to be my boyfriend."

All evening Fern sat by the phone in case Estelle's mother called.

` ` ` ` `

One morning, the following week, first period science class was ending when Fern began to feel strange. Instead of going to her next class, she went to the Girl's Room and checked herself. It was just as she feared. Now she would have to go to Mrs. Madison.

Mrs. Madison called Adele and arranged for Fern to go over. She was very formal. There was no question of someone accompanying her.

Only a few people were on the bus. No one was looking, no one could tell. She had cramps, but there was nothing wrong with her. Now she knew that she was normal.

Adele welcomed her warmly.

"You're a woman now! Sit down, I'll make you some hot chocolate. How do you feel?"

It's worth going through it, thought Fern: to sit in Adele's kitchen and be fussed over.

Adele brought out something from the closet and gave it to her. When she explained it, Fern understood. In the bathroom, Fern fastened it easily then looked at her face in the mirror. She didn't look any different.

"Are you all right?" her aunt asked from the other side of the door.

"Yes, fine," Fern answered. She reached for the knob and turned it, but the door didn't open. She pulled and jiggled, but the door wouldn't budge.

"What's the matter?" Adele asked.

"I'm all right," Fern said, "I'll be out in a minute."

Fern turned the knob more quietly; she didn't want her aunt to think she couldn't open a door! She sat down for a moment to catch her breath. It must be because I'm tired, she told herself. She tried again, but the door was stuck. She had to admit to Adele: she couldn't open the door!

"Fern, it's not your fault! The door gets stuck sometimes," Adele said. She suggested some maneuvers, but nothing worked.

It was too much. Fern started to cry.

"Sit down Fern. Try to relax. I was meaning to tell the super. I'm going to get him now. I'll be back soon."

Just when she was feeling better, she was locked in a bathroom! Ten minutes passed. What if something happened to Adele? No one else knew where she was.

There was a sound at the door - someone was there.

"Fern, we're here," her aunt said. "The super is going to get you out."

When the door was finally opened, Adele led her to the bedroom. "Rest for a while," she said as she closed the bedroom door.

Fern lay down on the bed and looked around. Heavy drapes were parted just enough for a soft light to suffuse the room. The fabric of the bedspread was the same as that of the curtains - a design of autumn leaves in rich colors. She had never been in the room before, had only peeked through a half-opened door. The bedspread was smooth and cool beneath her body. She wanted to stay in that room forever. She closed her eyes and drifted away.

It seemed but a moment later that she heard talking beyond the door. She was startled by her mother's laughter. Her own mother - laughing at her!

35

Ann had always felt bad about leaving college, so now that she had a job that gave benefits for a college degree, she started taking courses at night. She instructed Fern about what to do on Thursday nights.

"Salad in the refrigerator and make toasted cheese sandwiches," the note on the refrigerator read.

Fern made the sandwiches, put out the salad and called Don for supper. She had been doing it for a month and felt very capable. It was a cold, rainy night, and Leo came home later than usual. He took a rest and waited to eat with Ann when she would get home.

At 8:00 o'clock, he began to worry. "Did Ann call this afternoon?" he asked. Fern said she didn't.

"Maybe the trains were delayed, sometimes that happens when it rains," he reasoned.

Fern tried to do her homework but couldn't concentrate. Her father turned on the radio for the news, and a little later he called Grandma. He never called Grandma.

Finally at 8:45, Ann came home, flustered and apologetic.

"What happened ?" Leo demanded.

"Let me put my books down first. I'll tell you in a minute," Ann said.

"Why did you come home so late without even calling?" Leo demanded. Fern had never before heard her father raise his voice to her mother.

"Let's sit down," Ann said in a tired voice. "I can explain."

"I went to the library after class. I should have called, but I lost track of the time."

"That's no excuse for making us worry," Leo said.

" I lost track of the time. I have a history professor who said that six million Jews killed in the Holocaust was an exaggeration. Nobody objected, so I did. I think he's German, at least he has a German name."

Ann paused and continued, "I challenged him by asking to do my term paper about it. That's why I was so late; I went to the library after class."

"Doesn't he know the facts?" Fern asked. "He's a professor, he should know!"

Her parents looked startled, as if they had forgotten her.

"You're right, he should know, but some people don't want to accept it. At least he's letting me do my term paper on it, and I'll prove him wrong. I'm going to make him admit to the class he was wrong."

"Do we have relatives who were killed?" Fern asked.

"Yes, all Jews have relatives murdered by the Nazis. There were cousins of Grandma, but she doesn't like to talk about it."

Fern wanted to know more, she wanted to know everything. Over the next several months, Ann explained bits and pieces of her research: whole villages in Poland, massacres throughout Russia, the Warsaw Ghetto uprising, and round- ups of Jews throughout Europe.

Fern thought about the children. They were rounded up just like the adults, never understanding why. Those children didn't know they would never grow up.

The world was not basically good, nor were the people in it. Those fairy-tales she once loved were lies. For a long time, it was hard to get to sleep.

36

Two months before the end of school, representatives from the city's special high schools came to the Special Science Class to describe their schools and answer questions. The High School of Music and Art sounded perfect to Fern. Instead of science twice a day, it would be art. At the end of the talk, the man asked if anyone was interested. Fern was the only one. Everyone else wanted to go to the Bronx High School of Science, one of the best schools in the country.

The exam for "Music and Art" had two parts, an art test and a portfolio review. The portfolio had to demonstrate competence in pencil, charcoal, and paint. Because of her classes at the "Y," Fern had a good portfolio. She was grateful to her parents for that.

The day of the test, she took a bus and a train and then had to walk up an interminable flight of stairs through Morningside Park. Getting to the school was like climbing a mountain.

When Fern was halfway up, she saw a petite girl struggling with a huge portfolio. They both stopped to take a breath.

"Hi," Fern said, "it looks like we're going to the same place."

The girl answered, "If I ever get up these stairs! I'm Barbara."

Fern gestured towards the girl's portfolio. "That looks too heavy for you, mine is much smaller. We could trade until we get up the stairs. I don't mind."

"Really?" Barbara said, "Are you sure you wouldn't mind? I've been lugging this thing for two hours."

As they exchanged portfolios, Fern asked, "Where do you

live?" hoping it was the Bronx.

"Canarsie. And you?" Barbara said.

"Pelham Parkway, the Bronx. I don't even know where Canarsie is!"

"Way out in Brooklyn. My parents don't like the school in my neighborhood."

At the top of the stairs, they looked up and saw the school in front of them – a large, gray stone building with gargoyles and tall, narrow windows. It resembled a castle. Students with portfolios and musical instruments streamed towards the entrance. A limousine drew up to the curb, and a well-dressed girl got out. Holding a monogrammed leather portfolio, she strode confidently to the door. Fern wondered if she was a celebrity and why she would want to go to a public high school.

"Thanks so much, I hope I see you again," Barbara said as they parted at the door, each heading to their assigned rooms.

Maybe I've already made a friend, Fern hoped. She wouldn't see Estelle because she hadn't made the "S.P.s" and had another year of junior high.

The room Fern entered was an art studio, similar to the one at the "Y." The rich girl entered the room right after her, and they both handed their portfolios to teachers at the back of the room.

What chance do I have? Fern thought.

A girl in sweater and skirt posed as the applicants drew at their easels. Meanwhile, the teachers went through the portfolios.

After the test, Fern lingered to look around. It was an old building but well-kept. The bulletin boards had student art work better than any she had ever seen. Near the main office, she noticed an odd sign with the words "Bird Lives," in bright blue paint. She had seen the same sign on the wrought iron fence in front of the school and wondered what it meant.

By the time Fern got home she was exhausted and filled with doubt. She knew she did well, but there were others who were better. Ann told her to forget it. There was nothing to do about it now.

A month before school ended, there was an announcement in homeroom: "All students who were accepted to the High School of Music and Art please report to room 247 immediately."

When Fern stood up, the rest of the class turned and stared.

"Where are you going?" Mrs. Linder asked.

"I'm going to the meeting," Fern said to the astonished teacher.

When the results were in and she learned she had made Music and Art but not the Bronx High School of Science, she had been relieved. Her parents hadn't said anything. She didn't know whether they would approve of her going to "Music and Art."

At the meeting, there were twelve students, and she didn't know any of them. Then he came in - the boy from the bus! There was the flashing smile and the easy stride. It was him! They had been going to the same school all along.

A teacher instructed the group to introduce themselves and tell whether they were for music or art; if music, they were to say which instrument they played.

There was one other student, a boy, who was for art. All the others, including Jimmie, for that was his name, were for music. Jimmie played the base fiddle.

After the meeting, he came over to Fern and said he knew who she was, she was the girl on the bus. He had noticed her! She couldn't stop smiling.

"I guess you saw me getting on in the back. It's because I don't have a bus pass. If you live less than a mile away, you're supposed to walk."

"What kind of art do you do?" he asked. Fern told him about her lessons at the 92nd street "Y," and he was impressed.

At the end of the meeting, the teacher distributed a consent form for their parents to sign. As they left the room and headed in different directions, Jimmie asked if she was going to the dance. Fern hesitated - she knew nothing about a dance. Before she could answer, he called out, "I'll see you there."

After dinner that night, Fern met with her parents and told them how much she wanted to go to "Music and Art."

"You know you'll have to take a bus and a train to get there," her mother said, "and it's not in a good neighborhood."

Fern felt her heart drop. Would they refuse?

"What street is it on?" Leo asked.

"135th street, in Harlem," Ann said grimly, then turned to Fern and asked, "Are there any girls you know who are going? Maybe you can go with them."

Fern groaned inwardly - her parents didn't want her to go.

"How many girls were at the meeting?" Ann continued. When Fern said five, Ann exclaimed, "Only five from such a large school? It's probably because they don't want girls traveling to such a dangerous neighborhood."

It was during Science the next day that Fern was summoned to Mrs. Madison's office. Her classmates looked at her quizzically. Fern had a sinking feeling.

Mrs. Madison got right to the point. "You were on the borderline for the Bronx High School of Science. Would you like to take another test? You probably would get in because we'll give you a strong recommendation."

They had no idea how much she didn't want to "get in."

"I want to go to Music and Art. I want to be an artist, not a scientist."

"Are you sure? The Bronx High School of Science is one of the best schools in the country, maybe the best. I want you to think about it."

That afternoon, as she waited for the bus, a slight, blonde boy approached her.

"Hi, I'm Hal, I saw you at the meeting," he said. Just then the bus came, and he asked, "Can I sit with you?"

Fern was glad to have someone to sit with - it would be the first time in two years. They talked about Music and Art for a while, and then he asked, "How do you know Jimmie?" Fern explained, and he said: "Then you probably don't know he's like a celebrity. His father was on the running team in the Olympics."

"Is he a runner too?" Fern asked.

"He's a great basketball player," Hal said.

As Hal got off the bus at White Plains Road, he called out, "I'll look for you tomorrow."

The next day, Hal again sat next to her, and Fern asked why she had never seen him on the bus before. He explained that his father drove him to school on his way to work, and he usually stayed after school for band practice.

"How do you like Parkchester?" he asked. "Jimmie's family wanted to move there but they wouldn't let them, even though his father was in the Olympics."

"I hate Parkchester!" Fern said.

"Whoa!" Hal exclaimed, "that was unexpected.

"The problem with Parkchester," he said in a grown-up voice, "is that they want everyone to be the same." He paused, then added, "But in real life, everyone's different and that's actually a good thing."

37

For weeks, Fern heard girls buzzing about the school dance. They talked about who was going with whom, and she realized with a jolt they had already paired up. No one even asked if she was going.

Jill and Donna were going with boys from the class, both from Parkchester. Jill's 'date' was a nice-looking boy who was so quiet, Fern couldn't remember ever hearing him speak. Donna was going with a boy who had greasy hair and baggy pants. She didn't envy their choices and was sure the girls had arranged it themselves.

Fern started thinking about the boys in the class, boys to whom she had never before given a thought. There wasn't even one she would want to go with. Since it was at night, there was no way of getting there anyway.

Jimmie moved gracefully like her father; he probably knew how to dance. She wondered if he was as nice as he seemed. What would her parents say if she told them? Why were people called Black? Nobody was really black, just as no one was white. Skin came in all different shades and tones.

As Fern waited for the bus one afternoon, she watched students leaving the school. They were all in groups or with buddies. Then Hal came along. They talked non-stop on the bus home. She told him about the day of the Music and Art exam and how uncertain she had been afterwards.

"I wasn't worried about the exam because I'm the lead horn player in the band, and Mr. Bingham, he's the band leader, he told me I was a shoe-in," Hal said.

Fern told him about the girl in the limousine.

"There are rich kids from Manhattan who go to Music and Art. The school is so good, their parents figure it's as good or better than private school," Hal told her.

"Is the school mascot a bird?" she asked. "I saw lots of signs that said, "Bird Lives.'"

Hal laughed. "No, 'Bird Lives' is about Charlie Parker, the best sax player who ever lived. He's my hero. I'll never be that good, but I hope to get close. My dad is getting me a new sax when I start 'Music and Art. It's like the one Bird played. It's for my birthday - turns out my birthday is the first day of school."

The bus was approaching White Plains Road, but Hal made no move to get off. "I'll ride to your stop," he said.

"But won't that be far from your house? You'll have a long walk."

"I like to walk," he said. As they got off the bus, he asked if she was going to the dance. When Fern hesitated, he said, "I'll be on stage with the band, so wave to me."

Fern decided to ask Lina if she was going to the dance and if she could get a ride home with her. After almost two years of chaperoning, she felt entitled.

"Your mother will have to call my father," Lina said curtly. "But remember it's just to bring you home."

That night, Fern told her parents she had decided to go to the dance.

"It's at night, how will you get there?" Ann asked.

"I'll take the bus, and Lina's father will drive me home."

"Are you going with someone? I don't like the idea of you going alone at night."

"So you're saying I can't go?"

"Why do you want to go? Didn't you say you weren't going?"

"Can't Daddy take me there on the bus?"

"Daddy is tired when he gets home from work, especially on Friday."

"O.K. I won't go to the dance! And I'm not going to Marconi either. I'll just stay in the house and be a prisoner!"

Ann and Leo exchanged looks, and then Leo said he would take her. No one talked about it for the rest of the evening.

Fern was looking forward to wearing her Mexican skirt. She didn't ask for new shoes - it was enough her father agreed to take her.

` ` ` `

The high school acceptance letter was due in a few days, and Fern sat with her parents at the dining room table as if it was a formal conference. She said nothing about Mrs. Madison's offer. She knew it would complicate things. She wasn't as concerned about her mother as her father.

"I don't want her going through Harlem, it's too dangerous," Leo said. He spoke as if it was the final word.

"I wouldn't be going myself," Fern protested. "There are plenty of kids going the same way. There's a boy I know who gets on the bus at White Plains Road."

"Who is this boy?" Leo asked, and Fern explained about Hal.

"There are kids going from Pelham Parkway, from the north side," Ann added. "She can walk to White Plains Road and go with them."

Leo stood up, putting an end to the conversation. "I'm tired. We'll talk about it tomorrow."

"What if Daddy doesn't agree? Fern asked Ann. "There's no way I'm going to Marconi High School!"

"Your father is smarter than me, but he's indecisive. He sees both sides of every argument. I'll talk to him tomorrow."

All that day, Fern worried. She didn't want to end up at Enrico Marconi High School. After supper, Ann told her they had discussed it and decided she shouldn't go. It was too dangerous. "It won't be so bad. Your cousin Fernie liked Marconi."

"That's because she was a cheerleader. I would never be a cheerleader!"

Fern had expected her mother to prevail. At the least there

should have been more discussion about it.

Two days later, Mrs. Linder told the class that anyone who hadn't yet handed in their high school admission forms had to do it that day. The form was in an envelope clasped inside Fern's loose-leaf. At the end of class, Mrs. Linder asked for it. Fern handed it over. The teacher took it and put it in the top drawer of her desk. Fern hesitated. Was that it? Was it that simple?

On the bus going home, she thought of Langston Hughes' poem. "Hold fast to dreams/For if dreams die/ Life is a broken-winged bird/ That cannot fly."

꜀ ꜀ ꜀ ꜀ ꜀

On the evening of the dance, Fern was relieved there was no discussion; Leo took her and left her at the school door.

She stood at the entrance to the gym looking at the milling crowd. Everyone from Parkchester seemed to be there, some dancing and others in large groups. Then she saw Jimmie. He came through the crowd, smiling. From that moment things changed.

They talked as they danced, and he flashed his winning smile. She felt relaxed and happy. Then the music was interrupted by an announcement:

"February 3rd was the day the music died. Here's a tribute to Ritchie Valens, Buddy Holly, and the Big Bopper. They're watching from heaven."

There was a moment of silence. It was hard to believe that the three young singers, the top singers in the country, had all died in a plane crash, but it was in the headlines of every newspaper. Fern's favorite song was "Chantilly Lace" by the Big Bopper, and she too felt sad.

All at once, everyone started talking, and a group formed around Jimmie. The whole school seemed to know him. When the music began again, Fern was alone on the dance floor. She felt lost until Joey appeared and asked her to dance. When Lina came towards them, Fern wasannoyed. The night was just starting, and already she had to leave. In her brief time at the dance, Fern felt a part of something bigger than herself. She desperately wanted the feeling to last, but, too soon, it was ending.

Lina said, "My father is here to take us home. You have to come now."

"Can you give me a minute?" Fern asked. "I'll meet you in the lobby."

"Don't take long, I can't keep my father waiting."

Fern looked around for Jimmie. When she saw him in the middle of a group, he waved and shouted, "See you at Music and Art!" Hal was on the stage, and she waved good-bye to him too, then made her way to the lobby. When she got there, she was shocked to see Pamela and Kay.

"Pamela's father couldn't come, so they're going home with us," Lina said.

The other girls got in the car first. Fern wanted to squeeze in with them, but Lina said she would have to sit up front. Fern looked at Lina's tight-lipped father who stared straight ahead. She heard the girls giggle. They could have made room for her!

As the girls talked in the back, Fern stared ahead at the dark streets. They talked amongst themselves, not bothering to include her. She couldn't hear what they were saying until she heard her name.

"Fern, who was that blonde boy I saw you with at the bus stop?" Pamela said. "I was in the car and we passed by."

"I met him at the Music and Art meeting," Fern explained.

"He looks like a fairy nice boy," Pamela said with a giggle. There were more giggles from the other girls. If she could, Fern would have willingly gotten out of the car and walked home.

"How was the dance?" Ann asked when she got home, but Fern remained silent.

"You didn't want to go, what changed your mind?" Ann continued. "Who did you dance with?"

"I danced with Joey, and another boy."

"Who was the other boy?" Ann asked with interest.

"Someone I met there. Tall, dark, and handsome."

38

Ann said there was no need to go away for the summer now that they had a house with air-conditioning. Besides, they couldn't afford it. Fern didn't mind. It had been two years with no free time. Now there was endless time: time to read, time to think, time to do nothing.

She nestled into the sofa with a book. Occasionally she looked up to catch a glimpse of her mother in the kitchen. When Ann started singing, Fern stopped to listen. She had heard the song before; it was a tango her parents used to dance to.

"I touch your lips and all at once the sparks go flying/Those devil lips that know so well the art of lying"

Fern wondered if her mother was thinking how she danced with Leo when they first met.

"How old were you when you got married?" she called to her.

"Come into the kitchen where I don't have to yell," her mother responded, and Fern put the book down.

"I was 26. All my friends were married already, and I was still living at home, helping to support my mother." Ann laughed. " I was afraid of becoming an old maid."

The worst fate in life was being an old maid. "Pride and Prejudice," the book Fern was reading confirmed what she had long suspected. I'll never be an old maid, she vowed to herself, and inexplicably thought of Grandma.

"We haven't visited Grandma in a long time," she said.

"Daddy doesn't want me to go now that she moved to Soundview Houses," Ann said. "He thinks it's not safe. You know it's a low-income housing project."

"Does that mean we can't visit her again?"

"No! Nothing is going to stop me from visiting my mother," Ann exclaimed. "As soon as I get a new car, we'll go." The old car had broken down and Ann was saving for a new one.

Fern went back to her book and switched on a lamp as the light faded, but nothing happened. A minute later, Ann said the lights weren't working - it must be a power outage.

"It's a good thing uncle Sol bought this transistor radio. I never thought we'd need it," Ann said as they sat at the kitchen table and switched on the radio. Don came downstairs to join them, and they all listened as the announcer explained:

"I'm here on 42nd Street, reporting on the biggest ever power outage in New York City. City officials say it was caused by all the air-conditioners going at once."

" I hope they fix it soon," Ann said. "Daddy has to get home from work, and there'll be delays on the subway."

"What if Daddy can't get home?" Fern asked.

Consternation showed on Ann's face as she said, "If there's a power outage, the subways may not be running at all."

Night came, and Don went to bed. Ann and Fern remained at the candle-lit table waiting for Leo. If she weren't worried about her father, Fern thought she would enjoy the experience. It was like being in the 18th century.

At ten o'clock, Leo came home.

"It wasn't so bad, people behaved better than expected," he said with a wan smile.

"You must be exhausted," Ann exclaimed, hugging him. "What happened?"

"There were long lines for the buses. Then a woman fainted and I helped her out."

"A woman fainted?"

"An elderly lady, it was too hot for her. I helped carry her out and waited till an ambulance came."

The next day, the newspaper headline read: "The Lights Went Out, But New York Shined." Despite stereotypes about New Yorkers, people were kind and considerate, and there was no looting.

`   ` ` ` `

The letter arrived in August.

"What's this?" Ann said, holding it out to Fern. "A letter addressed to you from the High School of Music and Art?"

It was the moment Fern dreaded. "I'm not going to Marconi, I don't care what you say!"

"You didn't answer me!" Ann said angrily, handing Fern the envelope.

"It's my class assignment," Fern said when she opened the letter.

"How can that be? We agreed you were going to Marconi!"

"Why did I take art lessons at the 'Y'? What was the point of it?"

Ann didn't answer, and Fern continued. "For junior high you said I had to make my own decisions. I'm old enough now to make my own decisions."

Ann sank onto the sofa, uncharacteristically at a loss for words. After a few minutes she spoke.

"You signed the acceptance form yourself? Did you even think of Daddy, how upset he'll be? You make it sound like we're trying to punish you, but we're worried about your safety. It's a dangerous neighborhood!"

"But I told you about the boy who said he would go with me. Don't you remember?"

"Tell me again."

"His name is Hal. He lives on the other side of the parkway. He's going to meet me at the bus stop so we can go together."

Ann put the letter down and got a notepad from the kitchen. "What's his name? I want to get his phone number."

"Please, don't call," Fern pleaded.

"Why not?"

"I'm not a baby! It's embarrassing."

"Why should you be embarrassed? I'm sure his mother will be glad he has someone to go with too."

The next day, Ann told Fern that Hal's mother sounded very nice; she would talk to Leo that night.

The next morning, Fern was tense as her mother gave her the verdict.

"I spoke to Daddy," she said. "He wasn't happy about it, but I convinced him to let you try it out."

"Try it out? What does that mean?" Fern asked.

"It means we'll give it a year, and if it doesn't work out, if we think it's not a good arrangement, you'll transfer to a different school."

Fern thought about it for a while. A year was a long time. The main thing was going to Music and Art. She was happy, and she wasn't going to let worrying about the future spoil it.

"The High School of Music and Art" - all day she silently repeated it. It was like a poem she never tired of.

` ` ` ` `

A few days before school, Fern began a project. She spread her art supplies on the dining room table and sketched a birthday card for Hal.

Leo still hadn't said a word about Music and Art, and it was the evening before the first day of school. Fern watched as he read the evening paper. She waited for him to put it down and speak to her. She dreaded the talk, but as the minutes passed, she realized the paper was a shield. He wasn't going to talk to her. She was relieved but strangely disappointed.

The next morning, Fern was overwhelmed by what lay ahead. She almost forgot the small envelope with Hal's card, but now she slipped it into her notebook. A moment later, standing at the door, ready to leave, she took the card out for a last look. It had a sketch of the high school with a sign in front that read, "Bird Lives."

"Wait a minute, I have something for you. Here's five dollars," Ann said.

Fern was confused. It was too much money for a trip to school.

"It's in case you need it. Manhattan is a long way," Ann explained. "I have something else," she added, holding out a shiny black portfolio, the kind Fern always wanted.

Fern set down her old portfolio and gave her mother a hug.

"Now fill it with good things," Ann said.

It was the same walk along the parkway she had taken for two years, but this time things were different. The book-bag was gone, replaced by the new portfolio. The traffic didn't bother her, nor did the thought of old friends. And somebody was waiting for her at the bus stop.

It was overcast like that other first day. It had rained, and the sky was gray. The bark of the trees was dark and wet, but the leaves were a soft yellow. She tried to remember the colors, the whole scene. Someday she'd paint it.

THE END